Over and Above

Gurdon at Royal Military College, Sandhurst.

Over and Above

Captain **John E. Gurdon** DFC

GRUB STREET • LONDON

Published by
Grub Street
4 Rainham Close
London
SW11 6SS

A CIP record for this title is available from the British Library
ISBN-13: 978-1-911621-08-9

Cover design: Gary Blakeley and Daniele Roa, after a 1916
linoleum block poster by Harry Lawrence Gage
Text design: Gary Blakeley
Set in Akzidenz Grotesk and Caslon Book

Printed and bound by Finidr, Czech Republic

Contents

For Rob, Philip, and David,
the generation that links then and now

From the First Step to the Last Show

Over and Above was first published in early 1919, soon after its author, John Everard Gurdon, had been invalided out of the Royal Air Force following a brief but incident-filled stint as a flyer on the Western Front. Piloting the Bristol F.2b as a member of 22 Squadron, he scored his first victory on 2 April 1918, against a Fokker Dr.I. On August 13th, he snagged his twenty-eighth and final victory. He was twenty.

As is so often true, those months of combat shaped the man – both the best and the worst of him.

Gurdon was seconded to the Royal Flying Corps in May 1917 and that summer began flight training with 4 Squadron in Northolt. He seemed to love flying immediately, writing home, 'I have been up for an hour or so tonight in a dual control machine. The weather was splendid and the view magnificent. The instructors here are very nice fellows & very careful!!!!' The emphasis was no doubt intended for his mother.

By August 10th he had been confirmed in his rank of 2nd lieutenant. A crash during practice knocked him off the overseas roster, however, and he was posted to the flight training school at Netheravon, Wiltshire, as an instructor. The short passage from pupil to teacher reflects the speed with which young aviators were being trained for the RFC, as this air arm of the British army ramped up from four aeroplane squadrons at the start of hostilities to 150 by the time the Royal Air Force closed out the war as an independent service.

Gurdon had to cool his heels for longer than he wished because, as he noted in a letter to his father on 17 January 1918, the low casualty rate of Bristol pilots in France was restricting the demand for fresh pilots. But by the following month his turn came. On February 22nd, Gurdon senior's diary notes that Everard had been ordered to join 22 Squadron in northern France. There he was part of the very first flight of the newly formed RAF, on April 1st. Official war photographer David McLellan was sent to mark the event, and a famous group shot of the squadron shows a jaunty-looking Gurdon in the back row, leaning against the wing of an F.2b. *Over and Above* is essentially an account of the following few months.

As a fighter pilot, Gurdon earned some recognition for his part in what became known, almost mythically, as 'Two Against Twenty'. His and another Bristol Fighter were on offensive patrol on May 7th when they were attacked by a formation of seven enemy aircraft. After Gurdon shot down one, the German side was reinforced by two more formations, bringing their strength up to twenty. By the time the Bristols had exhausted their ammunition and broken off the engagement, only seven of the twenty hostile machines remained. An illustrated account of the incident was published in *The Sphere* on 29 June 1918; on August 3rd *The London Gazette* announced J.E. Gurdon's award of the Distinguished Flying Cross.

It seems that Gurdon and the other Bristol pilot in that dogfight, Alfred Atkey, were a formidable duo. The much-decorated fighter ace James McCudden recounted in his memoir *Flying Fury*, 'Atkey and Gurdon were at it again today. A parade [of German soldiers] was being organized (can't recall the town) and the two were diving on the festivities causing everyone to scatter in panic. Each time they regrouped they would reappear.' The town was Lille; no doubt its French occupants appreciated the show.

After a string of victories through May and June, Gurdon was shot in the left arm during a dogfight on July 10th that killed his observer. Two weeks later he was appointed flight commander with the rank of temporary captain, going on to score another seven victories, but in August he received a concussion from a nearby anti-aircraft shell explosion. The combined effect of these two injuries caused the squadron doctor to declare Gurdon unfit to fly, and he was sent back to England in September. By Christmas 1918 his physical condition caused him to relinquish his commission, though he was permitted to retain his captain's rank.

What was a fighter pilot to do when the fight had ended? This question preoccupies several of the characters in *Over and Above*. Certainly Gurdon struggled to make a living in the post-war world, although he was not short of skills. He had placed third of six hundred candidates in Sandhurst's Army Entrance Examination of June 1916 and, in a mystery now unsolvable after a century, was fully fluent in French and German. Family lore unsupported by hard evidence suggests that he spent some time in Dresden as a boy. It must have been for long enough to put his proficiency in German well beyond the average English schoolboy's.

In 1919 he joined the staff of *The Times* as a foreign sub-editor. There he was soon in correspondence with the notable Proust translator, C.K. Scott Montcrieff, over a commission to translate Georg Paul Neumann's official history of the Luftwaffe. Gurdon's English version of *Die Deutschen Luftstreitkräfte im Weltkriege* appeared in 1921, when he was just twenty-three; this impressive work represented an editorial feat as well as a linguistic one, for he had had to cut the unwieldy original text by two-thirds.

But Gurdon was a damaged man. While in the midst of translating what became *The German Air Force in the Great War*, he married Florence Mary (Molly) Pleming, the daughter of a retired Royal Navy chief engineer. She remembered Everard, as Gurdon was known to his family, sleeping with a loaded pistol beneath his pillow. He drank, heavily, and his diaries record that although he hated whisky he found he had to have it to calm his nerves.

By 1927, Everard and Molly had three sons, John, Philip, and David. Despite coming from generations of respectable lineage and moderate wealth on both sides, the couple lived at times in quite abject poverty. Everard appears to have been cut off by his father, possibly because of his drinking. He had already been declared bankrupt by 1925 and spent the next dozen years gradually paying off his creditors. Yet David recalls his father receiving a publishing advance and taking a taxi to the nearest pub. With his young family sometimes hungry, Everard would disappear for days at a time and return having poured away his small income.

His flying career had nonetheless given him material for almost a dozen novels and numerous aviation-themed short stories. With names such as 'The Flying Treasure!', 'Alarums Aloft', and 'Spies Fly High', most of these were in the boy's adventure vein, appearing regularly in *The Modern Boy* and *Air Stories*. But Gurdon also contributed to *The Strand*, the *London Evening News*, the *Times Literary Supplement*, *The Illustrated London News*, and anywhere else a jobbing writer could find column space.

Over and Above is different. Gurdon's first book, and arguably his best, it was reprinted repeatedly for two decades, variously titled *Winged Warriors* or *Wings of Death* and once even misidentifying the author on the cover as 'G.E. Gurdon'. The flap copy of that rushed edition bills it as an 'absorbing novel'. Somewhat breathily, the synopsis promises a roller coaster: 'Exciting raids over enemy lines and towns, desperate fights in the heavens against fearful odds, chivalry shown to an unchivalrous foe—these are the thrills which abound in the pages of this unusual book, which may justly be described as "the Beau Geste of the Air".'

It is not, in fact, a novel so much as a fictionalised account of Gurdon's own service flying career, with names changed and incidents rearranged. The book appeared less than a year after he left active service, and it is evident that he has gone to some lengths to shield the living family members of those whose deaths he chronicles.

The text is imbued with the studied casualness of an era and a class that put great store in maintaining a slangy, backslapping cheerfulness no matter how grim or bloody the context. Fellow airmen are chums who wish each other 'beaucoup Huns' before embarking on a show, in weather either beastly or topping.

But the narrative turns gradually darker as the men become wearier, new comrades arrive and are killed, and those who remain try to hold on to meaning in increasingly unintelligible circumstances. This trajectory no doubt followed Gurdon's own experience, and he passes it to Warton, the central character of *Over and Above*.

Gurdon had much in common with Warton. The beneficiary of some family advantage, young Everard was enrolled as a boarder at Tonbridge School in Kent, where he is listed among the house praepostors, or prefects, for 1915. Tonbridge becomes Mellbridge in *Over and Above*; on landing in France, the protagonist almost immediately bumps into a former schoolmate who reminds him that as 'a little chap in Eton collars' Warton had been his own 'jolly rotten fag'.

Gurdon's education continued at the Royal Military College, Sandhurst. There he excelled, winning a coveted Prize Cadetship and from the outset expressing his ambition to go in for the Royal Flying Corps.

While Everard was at Sandhurst he wrote often to his parents. Letters to Mary Gurdon were usually addressed to 'My Darling Mother' but occasionally led with an exuberant 'Ma-a-a-a-a!' Everard asked her to arrange for his weekend leave to include a party to see *Chu Chin Chow*, a comedic piece of musical theatre that premiered in the West End in August 1916. The play had an exotic Eastern theme, loosely based on *Ali Baba and the Forty Thieves*. If only notionally true to the setting, the bare-midriffed costumes – touted as 'very suitable to the sultry climate of old Bagdad' – must have titillated the eighteen-year-old Lance-Corporal Gurdon. One wonders if he later became disillusioned with these effervescent entertainments, as the theatre-going Warton does after time at the Front.

A letter from Everard to 'My Dearest Father' requests a portfolio for writing materials, six coloured handkerchiefs, and other required kit. Everard notes that he will have to acquire field boots when next in town but that he has already ordered riding breeches, offering assurances that the local military tailor is 'very good and moderate'. Such details echo the easy privilege manifested by the airmen of *Over and Above*, who down Heidsieck champagne and lay in stores of silk socks in Boulogne on their days off. No doubt the lives of the enlisted men in the trenches far below their soaring fighter craft were quite different.

Much as Warton displays some irritation at overpaying a taxi while on leave, Everard's letters often contain genteel pecuniary matters. Shortly before passing out of Sandhurst, he wrote to his mother to regretfully request £3 to cover the very heavy tipping of 'various serjeants, butlers, orderlies, etc.' that was customary on leaving, and noting that his luggage would also be excess. A letter not long after, sent from Central Flying School, Upavon, tells Mary Gurdon that he has used her cheque to buy goggles for a steep £2.5s.0d, though he insists he will settle the debt when his pay comes in.

The Gurdon family was also musical. Everard asked his mother to send sheet music to him at college to share with a fellow cadet with a fine voice. Among his effects is a programme of evening entertainment for which he wrote the music; he also offered a recitation and his sister, Myrtis, performed two dances. The scenes in *Over and Above* in which Warton and his observer, Lastor, are drafted in to make up the masculine numbers at a weekend house party while on leave in England clearly ring true to Gurdon's own experience. In the book, an evening of dancing is arranged for the final night of the visit, with the hostess at the piano and two violinists to accompany her as Warton attempts a foxtrot across the polished parquet.

This is not to underplay the more painful parts of the story, or their parallels in Gurdon's war. Within months of joining 22 Squadron, he was deeply affected by the death of his observer, James Scaramanga. A third of Gurdon's twenty-eight victories were scored with Scaramanga, over the course of a mere three weeks. On their last patrol together, on July 10th, they engaged in a dogfight in which Scaramanga was severely wounded and lost consciousness. With a Pfalz D.III coming in close on their tail, he recovered long enough to stand and shoot down the attacking aircraft, thus almost certainly saving Gurdon's life. James died of his wounds shortly after they landed but received no award – an omission that troubled Everard forever after.

Scaramanga makes his way into *Over and Above* in disguise, and we can only surmise how direct the links were in Gurdon's thinking. Warton forms a bond with his observer, Lastor, a laconic, witty kindred spirit who stocks his corner of their Nissen hut with volumes of French and English poetry and a silver candlestick. Warton and Lastor trade banter and share social assumptions, much as Gurdon and Scaramanga did. (Scaramanga's cousin was at Eton with Ian Fleming, and a tiff between them allegedly inspired the James Bond author to name his villain Scaramanga in *The Man with the Golden Gun*.)

But although Gurdon imbues Lastor with characteristics we can interpret as Scaramanga's, he does not assign him Scaramanga's death. For that he travels as far from type as he can – giving us Coote, a sergeant-observer whom the narrator patronises as 'a pleasant little man'. Coote naively shows Warton drawings done by his 'little nipper', as evidence of rare artistic ability. He keeps a piece of half-chewed string dangling from a corner of his mouth. But it is Coote who almost precisely enacts the heroic actions of Scaramanga, the hostile aircraft having been changed to a Fokker Dr.I triplane.

Gurdon draws more openly on his time in 22 Squadron to depict one of the most gruesome sequences in *Over and Above*. In Chapter V, 'The First Hun', Warton and Lastor are paired in a formation of four aircraft, another of which has Mellor as pilot and Dodge as observer. The day before has seen Warton and Lastor raid Mellor and Dodge's neighbouring hut to steal wood for their own hut's stove, Mellor having earlier pilfered a supply. Considerable high jinks ensue, reminding us that these are very young men.

The next day's show begins at dawn with Warton in a state of powerful excitement at the prospect of beaucoup Huns. These they duly meet, and Mellor and Dodge meet their end immersed in rippling fire. The narrator describes the blackened figure of Mellor, still alive, hurled away by the wind as he falls arm over arm into the vanishing point.

These appalling deaths mirror those of 22 Squadron pilot Fred Williams and observer Roland Critchley, both killed by burning on 2 April 1918, while on a patrol with Gurdon. On the same outing, Gurdon scored his first two victories. The mixture of exhilaration and palpable disgust that such harsh juxtapositions provoked in the young men who bore witness permeates *Over and Above*; its power cuts through the antiquated repartee to move us still, a hundred years later.

What must such experiences have done to Gurdon and others like him? After nearly two decades of hard scraping Everard left his family in 1940, initially to join the Royal Air Force Volunteer Reserve. He was granted a commission for the duration of hostilities. As a pilot officer he served as an instructor but also acted unofficially as a Wellington front gunner on several bombing operations – despite by this time being blind in one eye as a result of a 1935 car crash.

He relinquished his commission a year later after a landing accident exacerbated a hip injury incurred in the earlier motorcar crash. He also largely relinquished his marriage, leaving Molly living on hope, Catholicism, and not much else.

The second war took another toll. Everard and Molly's eldest son, always known as Rob, had joined the Merchant Navy at age sixteen before having second thoughts and signing on with the Royal Air Force. Sergeant John Robert Gurdon was killed in action on 11 April 1943, while posted to 166 Squadron. The Wellington on which he was air gunner/wireless operator was shot down returning from a raid, crashing in northern France not much more than a hundred kilometres from Vert-Galant, the aerodrome his father had flown out of twenty-five years before.

The middle son, Philip, was also involved in service flying. Joining up in 1941, as soon as he was old enough, he learned to fly in Saskatchewan under the British Commonwealth Air Training Plan. As a member of 273 Squadron, he flew Spitfires in Burma. After the war he had a forty-five-year career in commercial aviation but although he gloried in being a pilot, in its way aviation cast a long shadow. Rob's death caused Philip to be forever the elder son who should not have been, so perhaps it was a blessing that David, the youngest of Everard's sons, took a different path and did his service in the British army.

After leaving the air force Everard stayed in Liverpool, where he worked in a munitions factory for a time. While spending much of the 1950s and early '60s in the city, he met Vera Gaffron. She proved to be a caring and uncomplicated woman who, it seems, made him feel less burdened. Throughout those years he kept writing, shifting into travel books once his aviation stories were no longer current: *A Fortnight in Killarney and County Kerry*, a Rand McNally pocket guide titled *The South of France* and, in the Collins Holiday Guides series, *Switzerland*. These small books pack history, language, demographics, and culture into their pages with an impressive breadth of knowledge.

By about 1964 Gurdon's travel writing had led to a change of scenery. Everard and Vera drove their three-wheeled Messerschmitt KR200 bubble car to Italy, and stayed. The pilot clearly still inhabited Everard. Messerschmitt, temporarily banned from manufacturing aircraft after the war, had designed the small, frog-faced motor vehicle with a Perspex canopy that looked, and presumably felt, like an aircraft cockpit.

Molly was still in London, living in Hammersmith in a house that contained three small flats as well as her own. Her two surviving sons, Philip and David, had done their best to step into the breach left by Everard's desertion. Philip, my father, used his demobilisation money to pay for his share of the house on Marco Road, which the sons bought as a way to provide their mother with both a home and an income. She remained in it for almost forty years. And for several years Everard wrote to her, promising to return.

I knew John Everard Gurdon as an old man, living with Vera in a cramped and rather murky house in Alassio, on the Italian Riviera. In my memory he spent much of his day for preference in a checked dressing gown and corduroy slippers, in the company of an English terrier named, one suspects ironically, Bella.

This was 1971, two years before his death, when he would have been seventy-three. I was ten and had been schooled to be prepared for a distant man who was to be called Grandfather. The man who had left my grandmother and let down my father, and who was permanently short of cash and wine – both of which Philip supplied from time to time, rather bitterly. John Gurdon was, in some way both mysterious and yet powerfully clear to my childish self, not quite a good man.

And yet I realise now what an extraordinary life he had. Despite being wounded both inside and out by the first war, he volunteered and served in the second. He performed intensely brave acts. Even in his fifties he earned a spot on the Carnegie Hero Fund Trust roll of honour for 'heroic endeavour' in trying to save a drowning man. Although he suffered what now would be recognised as severe post-traumatic stress he managed a quite prolific writing career. As late as 1968, when he was seventy, he wrote a guide book to Florence full of pre-Internet detail that would have had to be painstakingly gathered.

Like all of us he was a complex figure, never fully knowable. Brave, weak, sometimes almost wilfully callous, at times brilliant. His life was deeply touched by war and by flight, as were those of so many of his generation. The gift – for his family and now for a renewed audience – is that he wrote it down.

Camilla Gurdon Blakeley

The First Step

Rain and the featureless clouds seemed to envelop the whole world; rain blown out before the wind like a thick curtain of gray beads, polishing the pavements, dripping from the roofs with a gurgle, and hissing as it pitted the surface of the sea. The boat rocked and rubbed herself affectionately against the quay, which was littered with stacks of case goods, coils of hawsers, chains, and piles of luggage. A few porters, with their coat collars turned up, lounged about, apparently doing nothing but shout unintelligible remarks at each other. In front of the low sheds that extended from the station along the quay, stood two rows of men in long khaki overcoats and webb equipment, waiting for the order to embark. There seemed to be hundreds, almost thousands of them, for the line continued as far as the eyes could reach. Some of the men were talking and laughing, whistling, or chewing sticky brown lumps of toffee that they fished out of paper bags; but the majority of them, in defiance of regulations, leant on the muzzles of their rifles, and stared resignedly at the rainy seascape.

The bustling and hunch-backed cranes slid along their rails into position for swinging netfuls of luggage down the hatches of the steamer. Gradually the confusion of objects lying alongside the boat was cleared away, and the men proceeded to embark. This they did with more whistling and singing, aided by monosyllabic barks from the N.C.O.'s. Each man, as he reached the top of the gangway, shifted his rifle sling more firmly on to his shoulder, and grinned at the red-hatted guardian, before he disappeared into the crowd within.

Owing to the rain, the saloon was crowded with officers–infantry, flying, and staff. Among the flying officers was one whose great size made him conspicuous. He was over six feet two in height, and broad in proportion, but his face was that of a boy of eighteen. Fair hair, blue eyes, and a fresh complexion, had earned for him at school the nickname of 'Fluffy,' a fact that he was most careful to conceal from the world. It was evident that he had no friends on board, for he made his way to the upper deck, where he stood by himself, leaning on the rail, watching the gangways being hauled ashore, and all the final preparations for departure. Then a bell rang, and the boat trembled as the propeller blades bit the water, while the gulf that separated her from the quay slowly widened. There was a half-hearted cheer from the men in answer to the few drenched civilians who stood waving on the jetty; but the rain soon came down between them and blotted out the land.

Towards the tall flying man leaning on the railing, there now strolled a short, thick-set subaltern, with 'Canada' written across the shoulder straps of his coat.

'Pretty bloodsome, isn't it?' remarked the new-comer cheerfully.

'Yes, worse,' replied the tall one.

'Thought you'd agree,' continued the other.

'The way the plug falls out of the heavenly cistern every time one's going back off leave, is enough to make you jump off the water-cart. Where did you stay? London?'

'Yes, I was there the last few days.'

'So was I. Not a bad place either, tho' the stores are so durned expensive. Guess it was built by a very tired man with a sty in his eye, tho'. The only thing that's up-to-date about London are its morals: and that's nothing to be proud of.'

'You seem a bit prejudiced against it.'

'Wal, every man's prejudiced against a place he's made a fool of himself in.'

'What did you do? Get into a taxi at Piccadilly Circus and ask to be taken to the Criterion?'

'Miles worse than that. I was coming into London from the north, and the train breezed through station after station, so I didn't have a chance of getting any grub. I had the railway box to myself and fell asleep. When I woke up, the train was standing at a long curved platform, and there was a refreshment room just opposite the carriage window. So I nipped out, bought some sandwiches, scuttled back to the compo, pulled down the blinds to keep people out. Time went on and nothing happened, and I was just getting desperate, when a guy, dressed like an admiral of the Siamese navy, poked his head in the door. "Train doesn't start for forty minutes," he said, "where are you for?" "Euston, London," I replied. At that he grinned a slow grin, and chuckled like he was gargling leeks. "Well! That's where ye are, and have been for the past half-hour," he said. So I cursed him, and made off feeling like a goll-darned gink just loosed from a Deficiency Home.—Now don't stand there laughing like a coyote. Cut out the rough stuff, man: cut it out! and come downstairs and have a drink.'

They picked out a path slowly through the scattered deck-chairs, some of whose occupants were overcome by sleep, and others by the sea. As they passed, a fat little man, whose shining field boots and gold-peaked cap proclaimed his exalted rank, rose unsteadily to his feet, and staggered to the railings. The Canadian watched his progress with a smile.

'How are the mighty fallen!' he said; then, losing his balance, rattled heavily down the ladder.

When they reached the saloon, the swaying stanchions, chattering glasses, and sickening throb of the engines, gave the Englishman a sympathetic feeling for the sufferers on deck.

'Don't think I'll trouble about a drink after all,' he said a trifle shakily.

'Nonsense,' returned his companion. 'It's just what you want. Make you feel no end gippy. Two whiskys and sodas, please, steward. By the way, my name's Bronchley. What's yours?'

'Warton.'

'First trip out, aren't you?'

'Yes. How did you tell?'

'Oh, you can't mistake the look. Kind of startled doe, lost sheep expression. I'm with "Toc" Squadron. Ah! here are the drinks. Cheero, and happy landings.'

'Cheero!–What are the Huns like now? Most of them are rabbits, aren't they?'

'You bet your life! All the same, I don't believe in taking liberties with a rabbit as long as he's got a machine-gun with him. There's only one kind of a Hun you can approach with perfect security, and he's a two-seater who's lost himself at six thousand feet, twenty miles our side of the lines, with a dead observer, dying pilot, two dud guns, and a conking engine. If you meet a Hun of that description go right up close and throw a stone at him. But treat all other enemy aircraft with suspicion. They may be hostile.'

'Thanks for your good advice,' said Warton with a laugh. 'There's not going to be any V.C. stunt about me. I intend to do my job thoroughly, but with a minimum of risk. You see, I've got another man's life to think of on two-seater fighters.'

'That's your bus, is it? I'm scouts. I wouldn't care to have a guy in the back seat. He might get killed.'

They sat talking for some time, mostly flying shop about crashes and different types of machines.

Meanwhile the boat rolled and pitched her way across the Channel. The soldiers on the lower deck, heavily bolstered about with life-saving waistcoats, sat round in small groups, scribbling postcards, or staring at the marbled foam on the sea. On either side, dimly sliding through the rain, could be seen the low, gray shapes of the escorting destroyers. Occasionally, above the confused murmur of wind and sea rose the piercing scream of a siren.

And so the time passed until the cliffs and harbour works of Boulogne loomed up ahead, when Warton and Bronchley appeared on deck, and joined the crowd of officers who were gazing with varying expressions of distaste at the dismal, rain-blurred shore.

'Well, here we are! Back to the jolly old land!' he remarked with assumed cheerfulness.

'Yes. And what's the betting there's a tender waiting all ready ticking over to rush me still farther into the wilderness?' returned his companion. 'Now where the devil's my bag? I told that gawk of a porter to put it near the funnel. Ah, there it is with a colonel-man sitting on it! Not so friendly, old sport.–Say, may I have my bag, sir?'

While he spoke, the boat, with much hooting and clanging of bells, was edging in towards the wharf. French porters in blue overalls and great agitation were standing on the shore yelling for patrons. A sergeant-major with awe-inspiring moustaches was waiting to receive the new arrivals. His dignity was magnificent until, in an endeavour to avoid collision with a travelling crane, he tripped over the rails, and got firmly wedged into a coil of rope.

The gangways were hauled on board, and the troops streamed ashore, to be formed up into platoons, and marched away.

'Thank the Lord, I'm not one of those poor devils,' said Warton, as he watched them go.

'Guess you're about right there,' answered the Canadian. 'I had two years in the infantry. Hi, porter! *J'ai deux* bags by the smoke-stack. Yes, my grandmother's quite well, thanks. Oh, stop your jabber! I'll take the damn things myself.'

When they stood on the wharf, he turned to Warton and said: 'Well, I expect there's a tender waiting for me, so I'll be getting a move on. So long. See you again some day.'

'Good-bye.'

Then Warton set about discovering his luggage. There was a large area close to the boat that had been roped off, and the kit was swung over in gigantic nets, and dumped into this square. A number of porters waded in and out among the bags, and tried to follow the directions of the officers who, ranged round the outside of the square, yelled vainly at them. After a long period of waiting, only enlivened by the complete disappearance of a porter who was overwhelmed by an avalanche of luggage from one of the cranes, Warton collected his kit, and put it on a barrow in charge of a venerable Frenchman, while he sought the office of an individual who concealed his identity behind a string of meaningless letters. At this office he was curtly informed that his train left at 12.30 a.m., and that he would forthwith report to another string of letters at the railway station.

The rain had stopped, and the clouds were beginning to lift as Warton, seated in a crazy old fiacre, rattled over the cobbles to the station; and when he had finished his business there and stacked his luggage in the cloak-room, he emerged to find the sun shining with dazzling brilliancy on the wet streets and dripping trees.

He stood irresolute for a few moments, and then wandered away towards the bridge that led into the business quarter of the town. Now that he was at leisure, and left to himself, he settled down into a state of contented depression. He reviewed the events of the day; the long period of waiting in the station at London; the strained remarks he had exchanged with his father concerning the vileness of the weather; the awkward silences: then London in the gray, wet dawn as the train steamed slowly through the suburbs; breakfast in the Pullman served by an irritatingly cheerful steward: he had alternately envied and pitied that steward; envied him because that night he would hear again the friendly roar of London; pitied him because he would miss the adventures and possibilities of France. He remembered the sodden fields of Kent that streamed past the blurred windows; the hours of waiting at Folkestone, during which he had wandered about the town buying magazines. Then the boat, and the cheerful friendliness of his Canadian acquaintance. Tomorrow that man would be going over the lines, and perhaps by the next day he would have been killed, wounded, or taken prisoner. How long would his own career last?

At this point, he almost collided with an old Frenchwoman who was hobbling along with a basket of vegetables, and he laughed to think how nearly his thoughts had been verging on the morbid. He must stop these sort of speculations. But the sight of a hospital ship in the harbour made him wonder how it would feel to be comfortably tucked away in a bunk, and bound for home.

He was surprised at the appearance of the town with its hurrying crowds, big shops, and electric trams. He had expected it to be different somehow. A large hotel styled the 'Brighton' caught his eye, and brought to his mind the fact that it was tea-time.

He entered, selected a small table in the lounge, and struggled to remember the French for buttered toast. However, the waiter solved this difficulty for him by asking, in perfect English, whether he would prefer his tea in the lounge or the winter-garden. Under the influence of food and civilised surroundings his spirits soon rose, and he laughed at the fears which had so recently oppressed him. As he was raising a cup of tea to his lips, a powerful hand smacked him on the back, and he heard a voice exclaim: 'Why! if it isn't the jolly old Fluffy one. Hallo, hallo, old sport! It gives me less pain to see your ugly face than it ever has before!'

Warton got up a trifle bewildered, and then smiled in recognition as he extended his hand.

'Well, I am glad to see you, Pat, old bean!' he said. 'What are you doing here? Just over too?'

'Just over! Good Lord, no! Half seas over at least! Going on leave to-morrow. This moke here's a friend of mine,' he continued, pushing forward a stolid and red-faced individual who had been standing uncomfortably to one side. 'This is Bunny, Fluffy. This is Fluffy, Bunny. And don't argue or mother will have to spank you.'

Warton and the stranger shook hands solemnly, while their introducer remarked in a falsetto voice: 'That's right, dears! I hope you two boys will be great chums.'

'Pat' was a good-looking lad with curly black hair, bright eyes, and a pleasant laugh. He formed a curious contrast to his companion whose freckled face was set in one changeless expression, and whose small dark eyes, fringed with light-coloured eyelashes, seemed to regard the world with supercilious dissatisfaction. They all three sat down at the tea-table, and Pat took up the conversation.

'So you're one of our gallant airmen, eh? Bunny and I are much humbler mokes, to wit–gunners. And to-morrow we depart for the giddy metropolis to paint it scarlet. Bunny has already started the painting business on his face. Buck up, Fluffy, with that tea, and get something to drink!'

'All in due time,' said Warton, 'my train doesn't leave till midnight, so we needn't be in a hurry.'

'Oh, you're just over are you, poor lad! And your little chow-chow leaves at midnight, does it? Poor lad, poor lad, two times! Of course, I forgot you were just a little chap in Eton collars when I left Mellbridge. Bunny, this gentleman and I were at school together! He was my fag, and a jolly rotten fag too. Always late with the hot water in the morning; always burnt the toast; always–I used to have to tan him three times a week! Would you believe it? But look what my example and careful training have done for him! Look what a fine young plant the grubby sprout has grown into! Pass the toast, please, Fluffy. Have you been down to Mellbridge lately?'

'I was down about a month ago. That young blighter Muggs is Captain of the School now.'

'The old order changeth, always for the worse. First me, then Fluffy, now–Muggs! Bring me dust and ashes, some one.'

So they sat smoking and talking until Pat suggested a stroll round the town. Up to this time, the solemn, red-haired Bunny had apparently taken no interest in life, and had only vouchsafed an occasional grunt in answer to the remarks addressed to him, but in the street his manner changed, and his small eyes roved round in constant inspection of the passing crowd. A girl wearing yellow boots and an enormous white boa caught his eye, and he smiled at her in so obvious a manner as to attract Pat's attention. 'Bunny!' he said severely, 'if you do that again I shall spank you. Fluffy, I apologise for this gentleman's behaviour. But it isn't really his fault. Under his dough-like exterior lies a heart of fire.'

'If they call thee reaper, whet thy scythe,' returned Bunny in a deep voice. 'You gave me a bad reputation, so I try to live up to it.'

'If you live up to it much more, old son, you'll never live to live it down again. And don't fling your tit-bits of learning at me in that pulpit voice of yours. On the whole, I think the only way to keep you out of mischief is to get some dinner somewhere. You're always more or less torpid after a good feed. How about the Leicester?'

They found the restaurant and settled down to a good dinner and a bottle of Heidsieck. As course after course disappeared, and glass after glass was emptied, a spirit of hilarity descended upon them: Bunny, even, became loquacious, and Warton remarked that active service was rather a good rag.

'And what type of bus are you going to fly, my young eagle?' asked Pat, 'A monoplane bullet with backward stagger, or a biplane cartridge with extensions on the fin? You see I know all your technical jargon. Talking of backward stagger, you ought to have seen Bunny after dinner last night. Oh, you were a shocking sight; you know you were, Bunny!'

Warton nearly doubled up with laughter at this. He thought he had never met such a pricelessly funny fellow as Pat.

'Myself, I pity our young friend here with the wings,' said Bunny, with the air of one about to make a good remark. 'If God purposes the destruction of an ant, he allows wings to grow upon her.'

Pat clapped a hand to his head in mock despair.

'There you go again! How often have I told you not to make those asinine remarks? They're an offence to the intellect.'

'They're nothing of the sort,' cried Bunny with some heat. 'That was an Arabian proverb.'

'I don't care if it was Arabian rag-time. It was jolly silly, anyway.'

Here Warton put a stop to the argument by leading the conversation into talk about leave and the London theatres. So they talked about musical comedy stars, and fighting on the ground and in the air; and how a second-loot made his brigadier feel small; and then about leave again.

'By the way, boy,' said Pat, 'when will you be getting leave?'

'Lord knows! In three or four months' time,' answered Warton.

'Well, don't forget when you are on leave, if you feel at a loose end, to run down to my place for a week or so. The mater would love to have you, and any one else you care to take along. You know my address at Maidenhead?'

'Thanks very much. Yes, I know it.'

It was now eleven o'clock, so they paid the bill, and set off for the station, laughing, talking, and feeling very happy indeed.

When they arrived there, everything appeared unusually funny. The porters in their blue overalls, and the apple-cheeked old woman who squatted by the entrance with a basketful of magazines, all seemed to have strayed out of a revue chorus. Even the tedious ceremony of obtaining the luggage from the cloak-room provided fresh food for laughter. It struck Warton that Pat had never been so witty before, and even Bunny, whom he had previously rather disliked, he now regarded with tolerant good humour. But the cold night air, and the melancholy sound of the little horns carried by the railwaymen, bit by bit damped the spirits of the trio. After waiting a long while on the platforms conversation dropped altogether. Warton was thoroughly depressed and sorry for himself. He regarded these two who were going to England next day with a feeling akin to animosity. Pat was thoughtlessly whistling a funeral march, and lashing at a piece of orange with his cane. Bunny was frankly anxious to get away and go to bed. The station was empty save for a few other officers, with their coat collars turned up and haversacks slung over their shoulders, who stood dismally under the glaring cones of light flung by the arc lamps.

Then the train jolted in, accompanied by much whistling and blowing of horns. Warton climbed up several feet of ladder, and secured himself a seat. 'We shan't be long now,' he said, as he scrambled down again. It happened that he was right, for shortly afterwards an excited individual ran the length of the train requesting people to take their seats. Warton shook hands hurriedly with his two companions.

'So long, you two,' he said, 'hope you have a good leave.'

'Good-bye. *Beaucoup* Huns!' As the train steamed out, he looked back down the platform. Bunny had already started to walk back towards the gates, but Pat stood in the light of a lamp, waving his stick.

Coming faintly on the night air Warton could just hear the words– 'Good luck!'

CHAPTER II

The First Flight

The drab gray light of a winter's dawn slowly revealed detail upon the obscurity of the compartment, as the image is developed in a photographic plate. There were four occupants, Warton and three New Zealanders. They all huddled in their respective corners, their heads sunk below the collars of their overcoats, their legs stretched out as far as the cramped spaces would permit, and their eyes closed in uneasy slumber. Hats, coats, haversacks, and bags overflowed from the narrow racks and lay scattered on the floor of the carriage. Dust covered the faded upholstery; dust, and the thick, paste-like mud that seemed to find its way everywhere. The air smelt strongly of damp clothing and stale tobacco smoke.

One of the New Zealanders was the first to wake, probably because a broken window allowed an icy draught to play over him. He yawned, stretched, cursed the train, the universe, the war, and himself in one comprehensive imprecation, and then searched fruitlessly in his pockets and haversack for a comb. Not finding one, he stirred up the man sitting opposite him with the toe of his boot. 'Got a comb, owl face?' he growled. The man, thus rudely awakened, grunted, opened one baleful eye, and glared at him. 'Nope!' he said, and settled down with a sigh for further sleep. After this rebuff his interrogator stroked his hair vaguely once or twice, and then came to the conclusion that a comb was absolutely essential. His eye fell on the large bag that stood on the rack over Warton's head, wandered away for a moment, and then returned to the bag. There must surely be a comb concealed in a bag of such pretensions. After what appeared to be a brief mental struggle, he rose to his feet with a determined air. Stepping with the utmost caution over the legs and other encumbrances that obstructed his path, he hoisted himself up with one foot on each seat, and felt for the fastenings of the bag. It was unlocked. He slipped his hand in through the opening, and groped round for a comb. Just as he was exploring the farthest recesses, and standing on tip-toe to reach them, the train gave a heavy jolt. Both his legs shot up in the air; he grabbed at the bag to save himself and brought it crashing down on Warton's head, before landing himself, a dead weight of twelve stone, on the stomach of his friend who was sleeping opposite. The latter gave utterance to a kind of deflated scream, and then gasped for breath to express his views on the incident. Warton awoke to find his bag resting upside down on his face, and most of his belongings lying in the mud on the floor.

For a time no one spoke, for the culprit who had caused all the trouble was too badly shaken to think of an excuse, and Warton was too bewildered to be able to do anything but gather the contents of his bag from off the floor and pack them again. It was the fourth member of the party, the only one who had in no wise suffered from the catastrophe, who broke the silence with a truculent demand for explanations. The first New Zealander told him to mind his —business, and then apologised to Warton for the damage. He explained how, in an endeavour to get a packet of sandwiches off the rack, he had lost his balance and pulled the bag down. After this he borrowed Warton's comb and peace was restored.

Meanwhile the sun had risen over the edge of the flat plain, and was climbing into a clear blue sky. Each man sat in his corner and stared morosely at the expanse of ploughed fields which were traversed by long straight roads, walled in on either side by poplar trees.

Warton felt thoroughly dirty and uncomfortable, and longed for a hot bath and change of clothing. If he could have seen himself, he would have considered this longing well justified, for his hair stood on end, his clothes were crumpled and soiled, and he badly needed a shave.

At about nine o'clock in the morning the train creaked its way to a standstill in front of a dilapidated shed which was evidently a wayside station. Across the roof, painted in large, white letters, were the words 'Le Condre'. Warton grabbed at his bag and coat and scrambled down on to the cinder track. A very ancient man wearing a peaked cap was the only occupant of the station. Assuming him to be the porter Warton went up and explained in halting French that he had a lot of luggage on the train. This piece of information did not seem to interest the old man in the least, for he spat with care and deliberation at a neighbouring puddle, champed his jaws slowly about a dozen times, and then swallowed with a great effort and further working of his facial muscles. Having finished these preliminaries to speech, he uttered a guttural sound and pointed to an office, adjoining the station, labelled R.T.O. Warton, wild with anxiety lest he should lose his luggage, dashed over to the office and woke up the sandy-haired Scotch corporal who was dozing over his ledger inside.

'So ye've lost your luggage, sirr!' remarked the corporal. 'Naw! naw! It wouldna be on this trrain. It'll be here to-morrow or mebbe next day. At ana rate,' he continued thoughtfully, 'ye ought a' see it aforr the end of the week.'

Resigned to the loss of his luggage, Warton next inquired the way to the Pilots' Pool. 'That'll be straight along this road here,' said the corporal slowly, 'aboot twa miles or mebbe four! At ana rrate call it seven kilometres.'

So Warton slung his haversack over his shoulders and set off, carrying the heavy bag with him. In spite of the discomfort of his long night journey, he had slept fairly well, and the cold morning air reinvigorated him, so he felt that he would quite enjoy the walk. There were several features of the landscape that attracted his attention; the roads running flush with the surrounding country without either ditch or hedge; the fields, also without boundaries, that resembled a patchwork in brown and green; and the little cottages standing up close to the road without so much as a pretence at a front garden. He passed through a small village, and thought it was very picturesque, with its broken-down walls of wood and clay, its moss-covered thatched roofs, and the uneven cobbled street. There was a small church too, whose surrounding cemetery was overgrown with weeds and grass, where the falling tombstones were pointing from every conceivable angle at the stunted yew trees.

A short distance past the church he came to a cross-roads, and was standing there debating which turning to take, when an R.F.C. lorry rumbled up, filling the village street like some sombre Juggernaut. He hailed the lorry, asked for a lift to the Pilots' Pool, and climbed up beside the driver. It was not long before they reached the officers' mess of the Pool. This consisted of a long, low, bungalow-like hut, with windows of oiled fabric. In front of the mess was a square patch of ground growing a few weedy vegetables, and on either side of this square, running from the mess down to the road, were two rows of Nissen huts. These were the officers' quarters. On the other side of the road was an aerodrome, and a great throng of buildings and hangars where machines were repaired, rebuilt, and tested. The surrounding country was open, bleak, and undulating, almost the only vegetation being the ubiquitous poplar trees.

When Warton got down from the lorry, he was surprised to find a pile of luggage lying outside one of the huts, and, on examination, discovered it was his own. How it had got there he never discovered, nor was he disposed to inquire, for its presence alone was sufficient to satisfy him.

He obtained an orderly, and chose a corner in one of the Nissen huts. Then while the orderly unpacked his kit, and set up his camp bed, he washed, shaved, changed his clothes, and went out to obtain some breakfast. After a hearty meal, he departed, with a cigarette between his lips, to report to the adjutant and discover what his duties might be. While he filled in the various forms at the orderly room, the adjutant explained to him that, beyond having to sign his name in the call-book once a day, his time was his own. He would stay at the Pool until a vacancy occurred in some squadron for him, and he might be posted the next day, or perhaps not till the end of the following week. It all depended on the weather, and the number of casualties. This feeling that he would have to step into a dead man's shoes did not please Warton at all, but at the same time he was anxious to get away.

There were about fifty officers at the Pool, and, owing to the rain, the cold, and the uninviting aspect of the country, most of them herded together in the small anteroom, and whiled away the hours reading, smoking, or playing cards. Every day some men left to join their squadrons and others arrived from England to take their places. It was a small community in a constant state of change, and, therefore, not conducive to the forming of friendships.

Warton, who was rather shy, never attempted to scrape an acquaintance with any one, and rarely spoke unless he was spoken to.

That evening, after dinner, he wrote his first letter home:

'DEAR DAD.– This is not half a bad place on the whole. I can't tell you where it is, but you may as well know that it is some distance behind the lines. You can just hear the

guns firing when the wind is blowing the right way. I had a
decent crossing, and was lucky enough to meet Pat Dower
in Boulogne. You remember I stayed with him once when
we were at Mellbridge. He was going on leave the next day,
lucky devil! The train journey down here was pretty beastly,
but I am quite comfortable now. We live in huts and do
nothing all day. The adjutant says I may be here some time,
as the casualties are very light just now. I think that a good
sign, don't you?

'There is no more news to give you, but I will write again
soon. You might send out some shaving soap. It seems rather
difficult to get out here.

'Your loving son,

'Jim.'

After finishing this, he went to bed. He found that he would have
only one stable companion, for the two other occupants of the hut
had left that day.

Warton had just settled down to sleep, when his companion
stumbled in. He was breathing heavily, and seemed to have some
difficulty in finding the way to his bed. When he reached it, he flung
himself down with a groan.

'Oh, Lord! Oh, Lord!' he said dismally. 'I do feel damned ill.
Everything's going round and round, and up and down. You're a
gentleman, old bean. You don't curse me. If you weren't a gentleman,
you would curse me. That's logic. Ha, ha. Q.E.D. You'd come over to my
bed and say, "You're drunk. Dishgushtingly drunk'n disorderly." Then
you'd curse me. And you'd be quite right, too, old bean. But you don't do
it. Therefore you're a gentleman. Simmons,' he continued, addressing
himself bitterly. 'John Simmons. You're in a beastly condition. You've
been drinking, John Simmons! And you've made yourself paralytic,
and a public nuisance. And there's a gentleman opposite laughing at

you, John Simmons. Tell him you're sorry, you old boo–boozer! Don't forget yourself so far as not to apologise to a gentleman for waking him up when he's sober. I'm beastly sorry, old bean; I am really. But, oh, Lord! I do feel bad!'

With another groan he turned over on his side, and fell fast asleep. Warton regarded him for a few minutes, wondering whether he ought to undress him. He got up, threw a couple of blankets and his own flying coat over the huddled figure on the bed. Then he turned in and blew out the light.

After lunch the next day, an orderly came up to him with a slip of paper on which was written:

'February, 1918.
  'To Lieut. J. Warton, Pilot.
  'Please note you have been posted to "Vic" Squadron, N^{th} Wing. When transport has been arranged, you will be informed.'

It was with something of a thrill that Warton read the little type-written slip. For a moment he stared at it smiling; then he crumpled it up in his hand, and strode over to his hut to pack his kit. As he worked, he whistled and sang snatches of music-hall songs. All the time, his mind was busy with speculations concerning 'Vic' Squadron, and its members, and, although he was in good spirits and eager to get there, underlying his jubilance was a certain element of that apprehension which oppresses all men about to join a new and critical community.

Having finished his packing, he went round to the adjutant's office to wind up his affairs there. Then, returning to his hut, he sat on his valise smoking, and listening for the sounds of transport on the road outside.

He had some time to wait, for it was six o'clock when an orderly came in and announced that a tender from 'Vic' Squadron had arrived for him. Within ten minutes he was sitting next to the driver, and bumping down the road that led from the Pilots' Pool.

It was to be a long drive. The light turned from gray to violet, and from violet to indigo as mile after mile of white road slipped by beneath the tender. Warton sat silent, wrapped in his thoughts, watching the two rows of poplar trees that fringed the road open out in front and flash by on either side. He felt lonely, desperately lonely, lost and afraid; not afraid of fighting or of being killed, but afraid of failing as a pilot, of making a fool of himself. He glanced sideways at the driver, half inclined to enter into conversation with him, but the man, his hands resting lightly on the wheel, was staring fixedly ahead, and seemed little disposed to talk. So Warton thrust his hands deeper into his pockets, and settled down to his thoughts again.

They stopped in a small town and he got an omelette and some red wine. Then, for the next hour, he slept while the tender continued its journey.

It was nearly ten o'clock when they turned off down a small side road, and the headlights revealed rows of lorries, cycles, and the other paraphernalia of an active service squadron lined up by the road. Looming huge and black against the sky on the right were the hangars, occasionally silhouetted vividly by the gun-flashes in the east. On the left were the Nissen huts that formed the officers' quarters and mess.

From the open door of the mess issued a triangular patch of light; and a deafening noise of singing and shouting showed that its inmates were in good spirits. Warton felt suddenly shy, and very unwilling to walk in on this crowd of strangers. He looked round for the tender driver, thinking to send him in with a message, but the tender was gone, and his kit was lying on the bank by the side of the road. It was clear that he would have to make his introduction himself. After a few minutes' hesitation, he walked quickly up to the door and looked in. It was difficult for him to see clearly owing to the light that dazzled his eyes and the smoke that filled the room, so he stood in the doorway, with eyes half closed, uncertain whom to address.

A man who turned towards the door to close it was the first to see him.

'Are you looking for any one?' he inquired.

'Yes. My name's Warton. I've come to report to the squadron.'

'Oh, splendid!' returned the other. 'Come inside, and take off your things. Major,' he went on, calling to the other end of the room, 'here's Warton, just turned up from the Pool.'

At that there was a momentary silence. Every one stopped talking or singing and glanced at him with curiosity and friendliness. Warton, feeling very embarrassed, busied himself hanging his coat and hat over the back of a chair.

Two men came over to him, one of them a major with a row of decorations under his wings, the other, a young lieutenant. The major shook hands with him. 'Glad to see you, Warton. Hope you had a decent drive over. Had some dinner, have you? Good. This,' he continued, indicating the lieutenant–'is Astley, our Recording Officer. He'll show you your hut and so on for to-night. You'd better come and see me in the office after breakfast in the morning. Meanwhile, have a drink. Two whiskys, please, Rhondha.'

The drinks were brought and they stood talking, while the rest of the mess resumed their interrupted singing and ragging. Warton decided he liked the major, and felt more at home.

But when Astley came in a little later and announced that his kit was being unpacked in his hut, he said good-night, and slipped out. The orderly had set up his camp bed for him, so, having undressed quickly, he was soon between the blankets and asleep. When he woke up, the hut was empty, but was littered with odds and ends of clothing, boots, and washing stands, and bore evidence to the fact that its inmates had only recently got up.

Warton glanced at his watch; nine o'clock.

He dressed hastily, fearing lest he should be late for breakfast, and hurried to the mess. The only man there was Astley.

'Morning,' said the latter as he entered. 'Had a good night? All the other fellows went up for a show at seven. Expect they'll be back soon. In fact, I believe they're here now,' he continued, as a faint drone made itself heard. 'I'll just dash out and get the news.'

Forgetting all about breakfast, Warton followed him, and ran across the road on to the aerodrome. About four thousand feet up, coming from the east, were five machines in close formation. A white light was fired; the formation broke up; and the pilots spiralled down and landed one by one.

Warton watched each one closely, wondering if he could land as well as they did.

Nothing of interest had happened on the patrol, and the pilots and observers soon left the aerodrome smoking cigarettes, to divest themselves of their flying clothes.

Warton then went round to the major's office and was told what was expected of him. Six landings with ballast in the back seat; a little firing on the target; one or two flights in formation; a trip round the lines to learn the country; and then he would be able to go on a war show.

After lunch that day, the major told him he could take up No. 5 machine and do his landings. As Warton went over to his hut to get his helmet and goggles, he was not encouraged by hearing one observer remark to another in the mess: 'This new chap Warton's just going up. Let's go out and watch him crash.'

To some pilots the period during which the engine is running on the ground to get warm is always tinged with anxiety. Warton had not experienced any such misgiving since the very early days of his flying, but this occasion seemed so momentous and fraught with possibilities, that he felt a queer sensation within him as though he were preparing to meet some shock.

Meanwhile the pilots and observers, but more particularly the latter, strolled on to the aerodrome and stood round waiting for his exhibition.

At last Warton slowly pushed open the throttle and the murmur of the engine swelled to a steady, satisfying roar, which died down to a murmur again as he signalled to the mechanics to remove the chocks from under the wheels.

The machine bumped round slowly until it faced the wind; then once again the engine roared, and the grass was blown flat by its blast of air, as the tail rose and the gap between the undercarriage and the ground slowly increased.

Once he was in the air his apprehension vanished, and a certain exultation filled him as he thrust his feet more firmly into the rudder-bar straps, and allowed his fingers to tighten affectionately round the joy-stick. The thunder of the engine was music to him, and the sting of the wind a caress. He dipped one wing until it pointed to the ground, and, as he eased the stick back and the nose of the machine swung round the horizon, rejoiced to feel that perfect balance of forces which goes to make a good turn. The aerodrome below looked much smaller than he had imagined. Like little chips of slate on a green cloth the hangars showed up against their background; and the Nissen huts like wrinkly grubs stood in two solemn rows behind them. A long straight road that resembled a chalk line drawn across the country passed one side of the aerodrome and disappeared into the mists of the horizon north and south. Warton wondered where it led to. He was to know every yard of that road before very long. The sky was heavy with sombre mist in the east, mist that was spangled with little flashing stars from the guns. Two rows of observation balloons floated motionless like enormous French beans.

While noticing these details, Warton was flinging the machine into turn after turn with perfect judgement and combination of stick and rudder. He knew they were good turns, and he hoped that the tiny black specks that stood in front of the hangars were watching him. After about ten minutes, he decided to come down and do his first landing. The wires sang gently as he spiralled down, and the earth seemed to be turned slowly round with the lower wing tip as a pivot. At a thousand feet he came out of the spiral and glided in a long, gentle turn round to the windward side of the aerodrome. Hangars, buildings, and fields rushed up towards him at a most disconcerting speed during the last five hundred feet of descent. He side-slipped steeply down over the edge of the aerodrome; thought he was going to fly into the ground; pulled the nose of the machine up sharply; and then the catastrophe happened. There was a jolt, a lurch, a terrifying sound of wood breaking, and everything came to a standstill.

Warton sat dazed for a few seconds staring at the wreckage. The undercarriage was buckled and twisted with one of its wheels sticking up through a great rent in the bottom plane. The wings were wrinkled like deformed things, and their bracing wires hung loose between the struts. The propeller, jagged and broken, had buried one blade in the ground; and the whole machine suggested, by its attitude, a camel about to kneel.

Wearily he climbed out of his seat, and stood miserable and dumb, waiting till the men running out from the hangars should reach him. The major was the first on the scene, breathless and very perturbed. 'Are you hurt, boy?' he said, looking Warton anxiously up and down for signs of an injury. 'You're not? Well, that's all right then. For a moment I thought you were going to kill yourself. You stalled her about ten feet up. Oh, don't worry about the machine. We wanted a new one, anyway. Those turns of yours were very good; very good indeed. But you want to practise a few landings.'

Warton was inarticulate with shame as he followed the major over to the mess, and he dared not face the amused glances of his brother officers who had come to admire the crash.

As soon as he was able to, he apologised to the major for making such an exhibition and breaking up a good machine by an ordinary dud landing.

'Oh, that's all right. You mustn't worry. Everybody does that sort of thing occasionally. Expect you got nervous with all those fellows watching you. Try again to-morrow. You'll be all right.'

Warton spent the remainder of the day moping round his hut, and trying to avoid human society. As he was sitting on his bed sucking gloomily at his pipe after dinner a man came in and started to undress. 'Funny thing, you doing that bus in this afternoon,' the new-comer remarked cheerfully, struggling with his bootlaces. 'Exactly the same thing as I did my first landing. It seems to be becoming quite the fashion. We'll be having a proverb. "Everybody who is anybody crashes on 'his first flip'."'

Warton laughed, and felt better. He learnt that the other's name was Savage, and that he had been with the squadron for over a month. After a little further conversation they both turned in and went to sleep.

A week later Warton had done his six landings, his firing on the target, and all his preliminary flying. He had also learnt the names of most men in the squadron, and something of their work; a few of the squadron songs; and the general routine of squadron life and thought. But he still considered himself a novice, and looked forward with mixed anticipation and dread to his first flight over the lines.

With the exception of half an hour's flying daily, his only occupation was to go out on to the aerodrome to watch the patrols take off and land. He used to stand rather shyly to one side and listen to the pilots and observers discussing the show as they stood round their machines. His spare time he used to spend in reading and playing the gramophone.

About ten days after his arrival a note came round to the squadron inviting all officers to attend a concert that was to be given in a neighbouring town. It was decided that a tender should be waiting at the mess, and that they should all rush down to the concert after the evening's patrol.

When the machines landed that evening, there was one missing from Warton's flight.

The major was standing in front of the sheds watching them come in.

'Hallo,' he said to Fories, the flight commander, 'Where's young Walters? He hasn't turned up here.'

'Oh, he's quite safe,' answered Fories. 'He turned back with a dud engine shortly after we crossed the lines. I expect he's forced landed somewhere down south. Pity he'll miss the concert. Come on, you fellows. Buck up and get ready. The tender's waiting.'

They all set out in great spirits, singing and making absurd jokes. What seemed to amuse them most was the thought of young Walters and how wild he would be at missing the show.

It was quite a good concert given by a number of girls, all of them, apparently, in the charge of an elderly and benevolent clergyman. Savage remarked to Warton that he was seriously thinking of giving up flying and going into the Church.

All the turns concluded amid noisy approval which would have warmed the heart of a London manager; but one girl in particular was applauded until the roof rang, and was obliged to come on again and again, each time to the accompaniment of more clapping, whistling, and stamping of feet. She was small, with fluffy yellow hair, and she sang with both hands folded in front of her, regarding the audience out of the corner of her eyes; or else she shook one finger at them in mock warning, although what she intended to warn them of was not obvious, for the chorus of her song ran:

'Oh, Mary had a little lamb,
With foot as black as soot,
And into Mary's bread and jam,
His sooty foot he put.'

Warton was greatly impressed by her charm. He was not sure whether she was 'IT' or 'O.K.' 'By Jove,' he said, turning to Savage, 'isn't she absolutely O.T.?'

'I wish you wouldn't drop your aitches,' answered Savage. But Warton did not hear him. He was too busy straining to catch another glimpse of the divinity.

After the concert they went to a small *estaminet*, where the food, though common, was well cooked, and the wine was good.

Then, with more laughing and scuffling they all packed themselves into the tender and set off for the aerodrome.

The driver apparently also considered the occasion a fit excuse for a little frolic, for the tender swerved about the road, flinging its occupants from side to side in a state of indescribable but happy confusion.

When they reached the camp, all the men rushed into the mess, stumbling and pushing through the door; all, that is to say, except the methodical Warton, who made his way to the hut, to get rid of his hat and coat. As he went, he hummed one of the tunes he had heard that evening, and thought what a lot of jolly good fellows there were in the squadron, and how much pleasanter it was to be in France than in England.

He was still humming when he returned to the mess. The major was talking and the men were standing round listening silently. Warton paused on the threshold as he heard him say: 'So it seems that young Walters got his engine running well again and went back over the lines to try and catch you people up! Anyway, he was some distance over when he got dropped on by a bunch of Huns, and went down. A fellow from "Don" Squadron saw him, and they rang up and told me. I'm afraid there's absolutely no hope for him. The machine was nothing but flames and smoke, and this fellow saw it burning on the ground for some time afterwards.'

There was silence for a few seconds; then Fories flung his hat and stick viciously into a corner. 'God!' he said. 'How damnable! Walters was such a stout kid! And he had Tommy Parker with him, too.'

'Yes,' assented the major slowly. 'It is bad, isn't it? Ah, well! Whom are you going to take with you in the morning? Is Warton ready yet?'

'Yes, Warton will do. We'll fly in pairs, and I'll take him with me and do a gentle show.' Just then the major noticed Warton standing in the doorway.

'Hallo, Warton,' he called out. 'Early rising for you in the morning. Fories is going to take you on a show. He'll tell you all about it to-morrow. Meanwhile, chaps, you'd all better get to bed. Leave ground at 7.30 ack emma. Good-night all!'

As Fories went out he turned to Warton and said: 'Your bus will be No. 4. I'll see you on the 'drome and tell you about the show then.'

Warton walked slowly back to his hut, thinking of the morning. He felt strangely elated, though anxious as to how he would behave.

When he had undressed, he took up a pencil and a sheet of note-paper. 'Don't think I'll write to-night,' he said to himself, putting them down again. 'Much better to say I've done my first show, than that I'm just going to do it.'

The First Show

It seemed but five minutes later that he woke up to find his batman shaking him respectfully by the shoulder.

"Arf-past six, sir. Leave ground at seven-thirty,' said the batman mechanically.

Dazed with sleep, Warton stared at the man, wondering vaguely why he should be disturbed at this hour.

"Arf-past six, sir.' He heard the voice half uncomprehendingly. 'Cap'n Fories sez 'e'd like to see you afore the show. Are you awake, sir? Or shall I wake you up again?'

Then, with a shock, Warton remembered. Of course, he was going over the lines that morning. He jumped suddenly out of bed, much to the batman's alarm, for he was not used to such a prompt answer to his summons.

'Yes, I'm awake all right,' he said in answer to the man's astonished expression.

There was a petrol can full of water standing near his wash-hand-stand, and as he lifted it to pour some out into the basin, he heard a sleepy voice from Savage's bed saying: 'Shouldn't wash before going up on a show, old man. Damn cold up on these blasted wintry mornings. It gives you frostbite. Oh, Lord! What a vile war!'

Savage sat up in bed, hurled a boot at his observer, who was sleeping at the other end of the hut, then disappeared like a jack-in-the-box beneath the blankets, and snored profoundly. A few seconds later he sat up again, and ducked just in time to avoid the return shot. 'Not so friendly, young man,' he murmured, retrieving his boot from behind the bed. 'Hurling other people's property about with your accustomed reckless grace and abandon. If I weren't so jolly good-tempered you'd rue the day you did the deed. Brrrr, isn't the cold perfectly —No! You're too young to hear my views on the subject.'

He slipped off his pyjama jacket, grabbed at his shirt, and disappeared into it, still keeping his legs under the blankets.

Meanwhile, Warton had finished dressing, had pulled on his long thigh boots, and was standing in front of a small, cracked mirror carefully brushing his hair.

Savage watched him thoughtfully. 'The dashing young aviator was always careful to preserve his debonair appearance while shooting down enemy aircraft,' he remarked sententiously. '*Vanitas vanitatum!* Lor! Lumme! I ain't 'arf froze!'

Having finished dressing, Warton went round to the flight commander's hut, and met Fories coming out. ''Morning, Warton,' said Fories. 'I forgot to tell you last night that Sergeant McEyre will be your observer for the present. He'll be going home soon, so I'll fix you up permanently later on. As to this show, there is only one thing to remember, and that is–stick close to me. If you do that, you'll be as safe as houses; but if you straggle behind, you'll probably bite it. We shall be flying in pairs, so you follow me out and we'll take off together. Anything you want to know?'

'No, thanks. I think I understand.'

'Good!' said Fories. 'Well, let's go in and get some brekker then.'

Somehow Warton suffered from lack of appetite during that meal.

He told himself that he was feeling a bit run down; yet he jumped every time a burst of firing from outside indicated that the observers were testing their guns in the gun pit.

Sergeant McEyre was waiting for him on the tarmac when he went over to the aerodrome, and the machines were drawn up in line twirling their propellers lazily. He exchanged a few words with the sergeant, climbed into his seat, and watched Fories struggling into his great fur coat. As he was running up the engine, Fories came over to his machine and stood on the plane, looking like a polar bear in a gale. Warton throttled back to hear what his flight commander had to say. 'Now, remember,' yelled Fories, 'stick close to me. And don't forget to load your gun.'

Of course he had forgotten to load it, but he rectified his mistake as soon as Fories had turned his back.

A few seconds later, the flight commander's machine, with two streamers flapping from its tail, turned away from the sheds and taxied out to the middle of the aerodrome. Warton followed, taking up his position just behind and to one side.

There was a short pause while both pilots settled down into their seats, arranged their goggles, and worked their fingers comfortably into their gauntlets, then, close together, the two machines skimmed across the aerodrome, and thundered up into the air.

Warton kept his eyes glued on the leader's machine. His right hand played constantly on the throttle, now gaining a few yards, now dropping behind, but always keeping close enough to read the number on the fin.

It was a fine morning with a fresh west wind. The mists were clearing away from the high ground, but still lay like wisps of cotton-wool along the river valleys.

At five thousand feet there was a layer of clouds broken into islands, and patches separated by narrow channels of blue.

The two machines picked their way between the clouds, climbing steadily until they reached the region of sunshine above. Before losing sight of the aerodrome, Warton had seen the other machines rising from the ground in pairs, but now they were above the clouds, he and his leader seemed to possess the sky to themselves.

Brilliant blue above, with a sun hard and dazzling, contrasted vividly with the soft beauty of the clouds, and the half-tone grays and greens of the distant earth. Looking over the side, Warton saw the shadow of his machine, surrounded by a rainbow-tinted halo, gliding swiftly over the white floor of mist. Glimpses of the earth, showing through the gaps, revealed tiny intaglios of villages and fields veined white by roads. Away to the north a patch of water, caught by the sun, shone like a silver snowflake.

But Warton was in no mood to appreciate the beauties of nature. He had seen them all before, and his mind was too concentrated on the machine in front to bestow any thought elsewhere.

He glanced round at his observer. The little man, with minute beads of ice covering the muffler bound round his mouth, was busying himself trying the magazines on his gun, and swinging the mounting from side to side.

For three-quarters of an hour they had been flying roughly south, but now, with a height of 14,000 feet, they turned into the eye of the sun, and flew due east.

Quite suddenly they reached the fringe of the cloud layer, and soared out over a region of air so clear that every detail of the ground below showed through it.

Still keeping one eye on the leader, Warton searched round the country for some landmark that he could pick out on the map. A long, straight canal leading into a town, and having on one side a rectangular reservoir, struck him as being an easy object, and he pulled out the map from behind the cross-bracing wires, where it had been tucked away. It was open at the wrong section. Holding the stick between his knees, he fumbled about with his heavy gauntlets, and endeavoured to open it. Although unsuccessful himself, a draught of air performed the task for him. The map unfurled with a great noise of flapping, leapt at his face, and wrapped itself affectionately round his head. He let go all the controls, and grabbed at the fugitive, which, however, whisked itself away and fluttered down out of sight behind the machine.

'Sulphur and brimstone,' growled Warton, and resigned himself to being completely lost for the rest of the patrol. If the worst comes to the worst, he would fly due west and trust to his observer.

When he looked round for his companion, he discovered him half a mile away, and nearly a thousand feet higher. Swearing softly to himself he opened the engine full out, and proceeded to climb back to his original position.

The ground below was pitted with shell-holes. When Warton first noticed it, the realisation came to him with a shock: the lines! Usually when a man sees the lines from the air for the first time, he experiences this shock. That ravaged, shell-torn strip of land is so hideous. Like some loathsome skin disease it scars the face of the country. To the east and to the west lie the smooth French fields; but between the two regions, scabrous and sprawling, are the lines. No matter how fair and sunny the day may be, the lines, brown and pock-marked, offend nature by their leering ugliness.

And to the man who flies, they acquire a significance only parallel to that of death, which divides life from the unknown. For west of the lines are home, friends, safety; but east of them lurk unknown terrors and destruction. The very country that harbours Germans seems contaminated by their presence; the trees bristle with hostility, the fields are smooth with treachery.

To say that these thoughts passed through Warton's mind would not be strictly true; but as he looked down and realised that beneath him all men were enemies, he felt like one who, swimming in deep water, sees the sinister form of a shark that watches him from below.

Later on, after months of flying and fighting round the lines, the full measure of their character came home to him; but at first sight they meant little more than a feature of the landscape that was both dangerous and fascinating. Yet he strained his ears to the sound of the engine, and edged yet closer in to his leader.

The first sign of hostility came in the form of a scalloped ball of black smoke that appeared with a sudden and vicious cough. Warton regarded the ball with great interest. 'Archie! By Gad!' he thought. As he watched the ball expand and trail its spume of smoke in the wind, there came another and another cough, each one closer and sharper. The leader turned round three-quarters of a circle, and dived some five hundred feet. Before Warton could follow him there came a tremendous 'crrr-UMPH!' from immediately behind. The machine shivered as though in fear, and, with a tearing sound, something burst through the right wing. 'Good God! We're hit,' thought Warton, and held his breath waiting for the engine to stop. But the engine maintained its steady purr, seeming to mock by its note of power the spitting Archie bursts. Then another terrible thought flashed through his mind– that his observer had been wounded. Half fearfully he glanced over his shoulder and sighed with relief to see by a steady movement of his lower jaw that McEyre was imperturbably chewing gum!

After the first five minutes, his nervousness left him, though his heart gave a sudden leap when he heard a quick 'rat-tat-tat-tat' from behind. But it was only his observer testing his gun. That seemed a good idea. Warton took a careful aim on a distant cloud and pressed his gun lever. The sharp rattle of shots, and the acrid smoke that filled his nostrils encouraged him as nothing else could have done. He hoped they would meet Huns and that there would be a fight. Meanwhile, Fories was turning and twisting, constantly changing direction and height, so that Warton was fully occupied with keeping in touch with him. He seemed to be looking for something. Suddenly the tail of his machine cocked itself up in the air, and he fell headlong away towards the clouds. In his anxiety to follow closely, Warton pushed the stick forward so violently that he was thrown forcibly against the safety belt, while McEyre was almost jerked out over the top plane. The machine gathered speed as the dive became steeper, and the wires howled and wailed, tearing their way through the air. Warton was standing up on the rudder-bar, trying vainly to see any signs of Huns. However, he fired a few shots as if to justify his dive. Fories pulled out and rushed upwards with the enormous momentum he had acquired, in a magnificent climbing turn. Not being ready for this Warton jerked the machine up so roughly that it groaned under the strain. Then he lost Fories. He turned round and round on a vertical bank, searching under the wings, under the tail, everywhere, for the missing leader. When he espied him again, Fories was in another dive, and at least three thousand feet below. There seemed to be a few black specks scattering east, but of that Warton was not sure.

He dived again and succeeded in joining Fories as the latter climbed. After a little more ferreting round, they turned and flew west over the clouds. Warton realised that they were going home, and wondered at the feeling of relief that came over him. On the whole he thought he had done well, but he greatly regretted those moments of confusion during which he had lost Fories and left him to dive alone. After the loss of his map, he had abandoned all attempts to follow the country, and so he admired all the more the manner in which Fories led, flying straight and unerringly for home, apparently picking his way from the meagre information afforded by the gaps in the clouds. Twenty minutes later, Fories shut off his engine, and commenced to glide down. Although the air was bumpy and disturbed immediately below the vapour, at three thousand feet it was so serene that, as Warton listened to the faint singing of the wires, he could have shouted from the keen joy of flying. Where the fragment of Archie had torn the wing, the fabric vibrated with a steady purring sound, and he laughed aloud as he looked at it. Far below, tiny figures could be seen working on the fields, and along the roads lorries, trailing a plume of dust behind, crawled in solemn procession between the poplar trees. A light fired from the leader's machine attracted his attention. Looking down, Warton could see the triangular green patch fringed by hangars and huts that stood for home. He spiralled down, swung into the wind, and skimmed over the ground. A couple of bounces told him that his landing had certainly not been perfect; but what was even a bad landing, he thought, compared with the fact that he had been over the lines?

Fories was standing by his machine struggling with an automatic lighter as Warton taxied up to the tarmac.

'That was quite a good effort, Warton,' he said as they met. 'Did you see those Huns we dived on? No? Well, you lost formation a bit there. Mustn't dive so steeply. Hallo! Got a chunk of Archie through the wing. Better examine that plane, flight sergeant. Let's go over to the mess. The other people have all landed.'

Feeling very satisfied with the praise he had won, Warton wandered along to his hut. Two pilots were talking outside the anteroom. 'Fories says that new fellow did quite well,' he heard one say. 'New fellow?' returned the other. 'Oh, you mean old Warts.' Warton smiled. It was better to be called 'Old Warts' than 'Young Fluffy'.

Dud Weather

There followed a period of rain during which clouds and wrack drove across the sky immediately overhead, while the air was filled with the sound of water, splashing in its puddles, rattling on the corrugated iron, and hissing in the furrowed fields. All the older members of the squadron accorded the weather an unfeigned welcome, but to Warton, new and enthusiastic, it seemed like a direct act of malice on the part of a Providence bent on thwarting his ambitions. Every morning as he woke up to hear the water trickling down outside his hut, he complained bitterly to Savage. 'Oh! Shurr-up!' Savage would reply. 'You have no feeling, no appreciation of the beauties of nature. Go to the door, thou unbeliever, and admire the nice wet rain wetting the nice wet landscape. Then say to yourself–"no early morning show to-day," and get back into bed. Before you've been out here a month, old son, you'll be getting housemaids' knees from praying for weather like this.'

But Warton remained unconvinced. 'It's all very well for you to talk. You've already got a couple of Huns. But I've done damn all,' he said gloomily, tapping his nails against the wall of the hut.

'Garn, you silly old croaker!' answered Savage. 'Here, "Little black dog!"' whistling to a diminutive terrier that always slept at the foot of his bed. 'Oh, he's a nice little beast, isn't he? You appreciate dud weather, eh! You lazy little swine. Come and do your morning exercises. On the word one! seize the animal's tail smartly in the right hand. Two! give the animal a brisk cant upwards at the same time bringing the left hand smartly across the muzzle.'

At this point there came an outraged yelp from the terrier.

'Oh, poor little beastie, then! Did he suffer from sciatica? Or has he strained his empennage? Here, Warts! Chuck over a bit of chocolate, or I shall forfeit Blackie's friendship for ever!'

'The way you ill-treat that poor beast,' said Warton laughing, 'is simply scandalous.'

'It's ill-treatin' the beast, I am; is it? Begorra! bedad! as they say in Scotland. Did you hear that, Blackie? Did you hear what seven foot of misery said about your master? You did, eh? Then seize him! Go on! See him off! That's right! Tear his pants! Pull 'em in the coal-bucket! Oh, well done, little dog! Well done! Now young Warton, you'll have to get out of bed and rescue your pants. They'll be on fire in a moment.'

Wearily Warton got up, pulled the endangered garments away from the fire, and flung them over the back of a chair.

'I was thinking of getting up, anyway,' he remarked, stretching his arms wide above his head. 'And, although you mayn't guess it, you're coming out of bed, too. And damn quick!'

He rushed at Savage, who buried himself under the blankets and clung desperately to the sides of his bed. There was a brief scuffle, during which clothes and pillows seemed suddenly to become animate, and leapt into the air. Then Warton rose to his feet, bearing in his arms a struggling bundle of blankets whence issued plaintive protests. This bundle he deposited with great care, upside down in the coal-box. After more struggling, in the course of which the coal-box was upset, the bundle unrolled itself and revealed Savage very much out of breath and covered in black dust.

'You brute!' he panted. 'You hulking great, coal-heaving, bully. You shall pay dearly for this outrage. I'll write home to the War Office, and tell them to give you the same decoration that munition strikers get. Then you'll feel a silly ass, won't you?'

On the whole, in spite of the rainy weather, Warton was not bored. Although he never enjoyed ragging round the mess, or forcing the broken-down old piano to groan under the spirit of ragtime, with a few exceptions, he was on good terms with the whole squadron. One of these exceptions was Gorfe. Having achieved some success in aerial fighting, and won for himself a decoration, Gorfe considered that in all matters, from flying to international politics, his decision should be final. One day, seeing Warton and Savage sucking lemon squashes in front of the bar, he strolled up and slapped Warton heartily on the shoulder. 'Hallo, young fellah-me-lad,' he remarked with patronising joviality. 'You giving drinks round? Mine's a mixed vermouth.'

'Right-o!' answered Warton, and turned to procure the drink.

'Old Fories tells me you've got on quite well with him,' continued Gorfe. 'Of course you lost formation a bit, but that doesn't matter. I've always been a bit of a lone star. Never worried about formation flying. Give me plenty of Huns to tackle, and I'm right there with some stunt. Of course, it isn't every one who can tackle Huns by himself. But if you practise looping and spinning and all the other silly ass tricks, you will turn out all right.'

Gorfe was celebrated for his displays of dangerous and violent flying round the aerodrome. 'Between ourselves,' said Savage quietly, 'I think Warton's more likely to turn out to be a fighting pilot than a music-hall turn.'

And, after that, the two men avoided each other as far as possible in the mess. 'Of course, he's a jolly stout fellow and all that,' Savage remarked afterwards. 'But ever since he got that ribbon he's been throwing his weight round. It takes some people like that. And his flying's awful. He ought to go on to scouts. Two-seaters are not good enough for him.'

A man to whom Warton had taken a great fancy was Ryeward. He observed for Savage, and shared a hut with the two of them. Somewhat weatherbeaten and grizzled, he seemed to justify by his appearance the Mons ribbon that he wore. Usually after dinner in the evening, if there were no special rag going on in the mess, they would stack up the fire in their hut, and smoke and talk till bedtime.

On one of these occasions, Ryeward, who was reading the paper, remarked, 'Isn't it sickening the way these fellows in England are always striking for something or other. Damn it all! haven't they got the imagination to sympathise with the poor devils out here who are getting shot and shelled to blazes all day?'

'They have not,' replied Savage. 'Sympathy is charity unapplied; and, with these fellows, charity begins at home, and ends with their union.'

'There was a young man of the Clyde,
Who flew in a temper and died,
    'Cause they told him he shirked,
    Tho' he said if he worked,
It was bad for his little inside.

When asked if he'd fight, this man said,
With a ca-canny shake of his head:
    "It's me for the benches;
    To hell with the trenches;
You can't go on strike when you're dead!"'

'Heigh-ho! As the first verse of my limerick told you, the gentleman is now dead; and the devil is a hard taskmaster!'

There was silence for several seconds; then Warton remarked, 'Why don't they bring these johnnies to their senses with a machine-gun?'

'Impossible, old bean,' replied Savage. 'Besides, it is contrary to the first principle of politics to bring a man with a vote to his senses. Now, listen to me while I sing you a squadron song.'

Savage leant back in his chair, and waved one hand lackadaisically in time to the music as he sang:

'Two Hunnische airmen voss Friedrich und me,
A pilot voss I, an observer voss he.
And vee used to spot for the artillery,
As vee sailed the skies in an old L.V.G.
Tra-la-la! Tra-la-la! As vee sailed the skies in an old L.V.G.
'Von day, unexpectedly, out of the sun,
An Englishman came with a synchronised gun;
And, after five seconds of glorious strife,
With a yell, poor old Friedrich departed this life.
Tra-la-la! Tra-la-la! With a yell poor old Friedrich departed
this life.

'On came the foe, with his guns spitting lead,
And, after a vhile, I got shot in the head.
But I never cried out, but I smiled instead,
For a funny sensation told me I voss dead!
Tra-la-la! Tra-la-la! A peculiar feeling told me I voss dead!

'So now vee sits up here in heaven above;
Our heads are in haloes, our hearts full of love.
And though they shot down poor old Friedrich und me,
Here's a jolly good luck to the old R.F.C.
Tra-la-la! Tra-la-la! Oh! I drink to the health of the old R.F.C.'

All three joined heartily in the chorus, and prolonged the last note in a hideous discord, which they maintained as long as there was any breath left in their lungs.

Ryeward got up and stuffed the newspaper vengefully into the fire. 'You've got a confoundedly nasty tongue, Savage,' he said. 'The question is, how much longer is this dud weather going to last? I'm getting sick of it.'

'So am I,' said Warton. And they both went to the door of the hut, and cast anxious eyes at the cloud-swept sky. Savage remained sitting with his hands thrust deep into his pockets, smiling at the fire.

The next day brought a new observer to the squadron. Lastor was his name. He already wore an observer's wing, having been out to France previously, so he was promptly admitted into the society of the older members of the squadron without having to undergo the customary period of probation. In appearance he somewhat resembled Warton, having very fair hair and regular features, but he was much shorter and very slightly built.

When Fories heard that the new-comer had been posted to his flight, he sent for Warton and said, 'You remember I promised you an observer to replace Sergeant McEyre? Well, here's the man.–By the way, I suppose you two have met already. No need for introductions, eh?–You'd better go round to the office, Warton, and show Lastor the lines on the map. He'll remember the country from his last trip. And the first fine day go up together and have a look round.'

From the first, Warton set out to make himself pleasant, for he believed in a certain degree of intimacy between a pilot and his observer. Lastor soon overcame his shyness, and showed that he could be both a clever and an amusing companion. He had his kit dumped in the spare corner of Warton's hut, and caused the batman to get busy making him a table, a chest of drawers, and some shelves for his books. Of these he had a great quantity, mostly volumes of English and French poetry. A few photographs, and a candlestick of silver trellis work that was attached to the wall by his bed, assisted to give his quarter an air of distinction. To a certain extent the individualities of their occupants were reflected by all four corners of the hut, but none to such a degree as Lastor's. Over his bed, Warton had fixed a large and brilliantly-coloured supplement from a periodical, depicting a British scout shooting down a German machine in flames. He used to assert that the flames were most realistic, until Savage suggested that they might be mistaken for orange peel. There were also a couple of Raphael Kirchner's drawings that dangled obliquely from the wall by one corner, and blew down behind his bed every time the door was opened. Savage's quarter was remarkable for its extreme neatness, and its only ornament was a card labelled 'Reserved,' that he had stolen from the stalls of a London theatre. Above the bed of that taciturn old campaigner, Ryeward, there hung a battered tin helmet, and a German bayonet whose scabbard was rotted by damp and age.

In addition to their personal belongings the hut boasted of several pieces of furniture; a rickety table hewn from a bomb box stood in the middle of the room; an iron stove that consumed an enormous quantity of wood occupied one end, and at the other end of the hut, a complicated system of canvas screens protected the inmates from the draughty door. Long clothes lines, usually composed of bootlaces, tied together, hung across the roof, groaning under the weight of clothes they were required to bear. Periodically the lines snapped, and the resulting litter on the floor was kicked into a corner, at what time the batman ferreted round the camp for more bootlaces. An acetylene generator swung between two flimsy wires attached to the ceiling, but it was never used, because Savage complained that he hated sleeping in a gas-mask.

Candles, therefore, were substituted as an illuminant, and, as Lastor possessed the only candlestick, the table was always covered with degraded stumps wallowing in congealed pools of wax.

There was always a difficulty in obtaining fuel for the stove.

Occasionally it was possible to get a sack of inferior coke from the nearest village, but such windfalls were of infrequent occurrence and not to be relied on. However, the squadron that lived at an aerodrome half a mile down the road had collected for itself a large supply of empty bomb boxes, and had unwisely left these boxes stacked by the wayside. Although the dump was jealously guarded, it was discovered that by engaging the sentry with conversation and cigarettes, two or three boxes could be quietly removed and hurried away in a tender.

It was after one of these raids that Warton discovered an enormous wooden case in the hut of Mellor and Dodge, who lived next door. He acquainted Lastor with his discovery. 'Those dishonest ruffians next door,' he said, 'have been pinching other people's property. They've got a huge empty bomb box in there. What shall we do about it?'

'You shock me greatly!' answered Lastor piously. 'That men can do such things! I vote we bag the box and use it ourselves.'

'That is obviously our duty,' said Warton.

'I wouldn't like those fellows to get into a row through having stolen property discovered in their apartments. The trouble is that Mellor's in there now.'

'Well, let's send Ryeward in with a message saying that the C.O. wants to speak to Mellor.'

'Good idea! Here, Ryeward. Wake up!'

'Wha's the matter?' grunted Ryeward, who was lying on his bed overcome by sleep.

'Wake up, man! And go in to Mellor next door and say the C.O. wants to speak to him.'

Ryeward blinked dazedly at the speaker before replying. 'Do you mean to tell me you woke a poor hard-working bloke up to make him carry messages for you? Why the devil don't you do your own dirty work?'

'The answer's a bomb box,' said Warton.

It took some time to explain the situation to Ryeward, but eventually he departed grumbling to deliver his message, and shortly afterwards the two conspirators heard Mellor as he splashed his way through the mud to the squadron office.

'Now's the time,' whispered Warton. As soon as Ryeward returned, they slipped out and peered into Mellor's hut, through a crack in the door. It was empty, and the bomb box stood challenging them from its position near the stove.

'Good enough!' said Lastor. 'Now for our jolly old firewood. You wedge the door open, Warts, while I drag the box over.'

Warton thrust a peg of wood in under the door, kicked it well home, and went over to assist Lastor. It was a large box, open down one side, and measuring very nearly six foot by three. They had just laid hands on it when from outside came unmistakable sounds of footsteps approaching the hut.

'Good Lord! There's Mellor!' murmured Lastor feebly. 'Dash over, and shut the door, Warts!'

Warton leapt for the door and endeavoured to slam it to. But the peg of wood with which he had wedged it open frustrated his efforts, and he was still struggling when Mellor appeared on the threshold. At the same moment there came a bang on the floor from behind, as if the bomb box had fallen over.

'Hallo, Warton,' said Mellor pleasantly. 'Come to pay me a little visit, eh? Not that I flatter myself you called entirely on my account. Perhaps you just popped in to have a look at my recent acquisition: boxes, wooden, large, bombs, for the use of, primarily; officers' stove, for the use of, secondarily. Hallo! What a funny chap you are! Been wedging my door open! One would almost think you had some nefarious business on hand. Never mind; leave it open. There's a bit of a fug in the hut.'

While making these remarks Mellor had strolled over to his bed, where he flung himself down and lit a cigarette.

'Come in, Warton!' he called out. 'Make yourself at home, and tell me to what I am indebted for the honour of your presence.'

Warton, very confused and tongue-tied, entered and sat down. The bomb box, which had previously been standing on end, was lying at full length on the floor with its open side downwards. And Lastor had completely disappeared. While Warton's mind was busy trying to explain these phenomena, and Mellor was blowing smoke rings at the ceiling and chatting amiably, he was amazed to see the bomb box slowly move towards the door. There could be no doubt about it. Warton watched in fascinated suspense while the box negotiated a difficult corner by the wash-hand-stand, and then scuttled rapidly over the last straight lap that led to freedom. As it reached the door, it rose up on end, and Warton caught a glimpse of two trouser-clad legs beneath, before it vanished into the night. Meanwhile Mellor was still talking. 'Do you know, old man,' he was saying, 'I admire your skill as an amateur cracksman. That bogus message from the C.O. was a veritable brain-wave. Luckily, I met the C.O. just coming out of the mess, otherwise you would probably have got clear away with the dibs, leaving me destitute of firewood for another week. What? You can't stay? Well, then, close the door after you. And better luck next time!'

Warton left him chuckling, and still blowing smoke-rings at the ceiling.

When he reached his own hut, he found Lastor, very dusty, and helpless with laughter, sitting on the captured bomb box. 'Very good indeed!' said Warton, slapping him heartily on the back. 'D'you know, I didn't have the vaguest idea where you had got to!'

'Here! Steady with your physical manifestations of joy!' Lastor replied, gasping for breath. 'By Jove, though! Didn't we do old Mellor in properly! By a stroke of luck, there was a hole in one side, so I could just see where I was going. Now, then, if you jamb the door so's the outraged Mellor can't get in, we'll break up our trophy and get a rattling good fire going.'

Shortly afterwards, Savage came in, and the quartet drew their chairs close round the stove, with all the keener zest because they were enjoying stolen fruit. Yet somehow Warton felt uncomfortable, as though he were travelling first class with a third class ticket.

'I say!' he suddenly broke out. 'Don't you think we ought to let Mellor in? There's a regular frost in his hut.'

'Isn't that rather like stealing sixpence out of a blind man's hat and giving him back a ha'penny?' laughed Savage.

'Yes,' continued Warton awkwardly. 'But I was thinking–don't you chaps think we ought to give him back half his wood? After all, he got the box, you know!'

Ryeward grunted contemptuously. 'Mellor pinched the box from total strangers,' he said, 'whereas we only pinched it from a friend. There's a lot of difference between the two.'

'Don't think much of your morals,' said Savage. 'That accounts for a lot of the things I've lost recently. As a matter of fact I quite agree with Warts. I think we ought to give Mellor some of this firewood.'

'So do I,' agreed Lastor.

'Oh! Very well, then,' said Ryeward impatiently. 'Give him the wood. Give him the lot! Give him the whole beastly hut! I don't care!'

'That's a good boy!' Savage answered soothingly. 'I knew mother's pet would be polite. I'll go and ask Mellor in.'

When Mellor first entered he was inclined to be hostile, but he soon thawed, laughed at Lastor's humorous account of the theft, and said he would be content to share the wood.

For a time the five men sat silently round the fire. Then Ryeward shifted his chair nearer to the blaze. 'Huh!' he said. 'Give me some chestnuts now, and I'll stay out in France for the duration.'

On the sixth day of the rainy weather, Gorfe left the squadron for home. The usual group of envious ones gathered round the tender that was to carry him to Boulogne. Gorfe, resplendent in a new uniform, stood in the centre of the group shaking hands with everybody and wishing them luck. When he came to Warton, he reached up to lay a hand in mock blessing on his head.

'Mark well my words,' he intoned in a solemn voice. 'Some day this stripling will be a fighting pilot.'

As the tender jerked itself away, and splashed down the muddy road there came a chorus of 'Good lucks!' from the onlookers, and a fountain of Very lights hissed into the air, describing parabolas of vivid colour against the sky. Warton watched the last light spluttering out on the wet grass before turning back to the mess.

'Lucky devil!' he sighed. 'This time to-morrow, he'll be home.'

'Yes!' assented Savage. 'And this time next month he'll be instructing in some God-forsaken hole on Salisbury Plain, and wishing every hour he could get back to France.'

That evening the clouds rolled away, and the sun set in an orgy of gold that deepened and faded as night drew on. The moon rose, throwing a thin film of silver over the fields, and multiplying itself in a thousand and one patches of water.

Warton came across Lastor leaning up against the door of his hut.

'Topping night, isn't it?' he remarked cheerfully. 'What's the betting friend Hoggenheimer comes over and drops high explosives on us?'

'Shouldn't be surprised,' said Lastor. 'I was just thinking how the moon shining through the branches of that tree looks exactly like a Japanese screen we've got at home. I remember, too, a night like this in Spain when I went to see the Alhambra, and—'

'What's that about the Alhambra?' said a deep voice, and Ryeward pushed past them into the hut. 'I always go to the Hippo, myself. There's an early show in the morning. I say, Warton, lend us your towel. I've just got in a filthy mess cleaning my gun.'

'Use your own towel,' shouted Warton.

'Can't!' came the voice from within, muffled by a sound of vigorous rubbing. 'One's in the wash, and that fool, Budge, used the other to wipe the floor with.'

Savage was in great spirits at the thought of flying the next day, and he kept his companions in fits of laughter, while they were going to bed, by lying flat on his stomach and stalking an earwig that was meandering across the room.

'The best way of stalking these animals,' he whispered, 'is to crawl up behind them making a noise like a precipice. The beast gets frightened, falls over the edge of the precipice, and breaks his blasted neck! Ah-ha! He's scented me! See him shake his feelers at me? Now, having got the enemy on the run, we press upon his rear, so–with a pencil. On you get, you ugly monster! On, I say! Up the wall! Stop arguing!'

The bewildered earwig eventually came to a standstill on the German bayonet that hung over Ryeward's bed, and tested the air querulously with its feelers.

'Now we've got you!' said Savage triumphantly, rolling up his shirt-sleeves. 'Now, you're about to meet a sticky end, you caddish nut-brown armour-plated interloper!' he continued, selecting a hob-nailed boot from under his bed. 'You hairy, horrible Hun! I say, chaps, I believe this insect's the Crown Prince in disguise! Look at his chin! Anyway, here goes! One! Two! Three! Bang!'

A well-aimed boot hit the bayonet and corrugated iron with a noise like a big gun exploding. The bayonet fell off the wall with a clatter, and Ryeward, who was just getting into bed, was liberally sprinkled with a shower of iron rust.

'Here! What the deuce do you think you're doing?' he demanded fiercely. 'There's about half a ton of dust and spiders down the back of my pyjamas.'

'Sorry, old man!' said Savage lightly. 'I was just bringing a Hun down out of control. See! Here he is crashed, a complete write-off, on the end of your skewer.'

'Oh, put the confounded bayonet down!' growled Ryeward, trying vainly to reach between his shoulder blades.

'By the way,' said Savage, drawing the blade from its sheath. 'This is a Hun bayonet, isn't it? How'd you get it? By honest fighting or by wangling?'

'What do you mean "by wangling"?' Ryeward asked, stopping his scratching for a moment.

Savage turned his eyes upwards.

'Wangling, oh, my dearly beloved brethren,' he said, 'is the art of getting what you want without getting what you deserve.'

'Shut up, and go to bed!' growled Ryeward. 'There's an early show in the morning. You're too darned funny!'

The First Hun

Clear skies welcomed the sun, and with the first rays of light came a stir and activity in the camp. From time to time the silence was broken by a muffled roar as the mechanics tested their engines on the aerodrome, and along the cinder paths that wound in and out of the officers' quarters, batmen hurried with cups of steaming tea. One by one, figures clad in heavy leather and fur emerged from the huts and tramped wearily to the mess, where they swallowed a hastily-prepared breakfast and discoursed in monosyllables.

Fories, with the collar of his coat turned up to his ears, was staring moodily at an empty plate when Warton entered. ''Morning, Warton,' he said. 'You'll have the same bus as you had last time. Does Lastor know he's on this show with you? He does? Good! There'll be four of us to-day. Mellor and Savage are coming too. You take the tail of the formation. Stick close, and if you can't keep up for some reason, dive down underneath the rest and stay there. You'll be safe there. Orderly! How much longer are you going to be getting that egg and bacon?'

Warton ate his breakfast with a hearty appetite. He was looking forward to this show, and felt instinctively that Lastor was a good man to have in the back seat.

As they both walked over to the aerodrome he remarked:

'Gad! I hope we meet some perfectly good Huns this morning. Do you think we shall?'

'Bound to,' answered Lastor laconically. 'They always come out in the morning when the sun's in their favour.'

It was the first time that Warton had realised that Lastor was an experienced fighter. 'Have you got any Huns?' he asked, with new interest.

'Yep! Three,' replied Lastor. And from that moment Warton regarded his observer with respect.

When the four machines taxied out and took up their formation on the ground, Warton could hardly keep still from anxiety to be off. He sat biting the fingers of his gauntlet, and thought with regret of the time they would have to spend gaining height before crossing the lines. So occupied was he with his thoughts that he failed to see the leader's observer stand up and wave his arms in signal that they were about to take off. The other machines had already started to move slowly over the ground before his hand touched the throttle. Then he pushed the lever open sharply, and was irritated when the engine protested with a choke and splutter. He dropped behind, took off badly with his tail still on the ground, and flew straight into the slip-stream caused by Savage in front. His machine staggered under the heavy blast of air, and almost side-slipped into the ground, but he pulled the wing up quickly, and climbed to his position in formation.

Trifling though this incident had been, it worried him considerably, for the major, who was standing in front of his office, must have seen it. However, as his mind became concentrated on flying, the irritation wore off and was gradually forgotten.

The promise of fair weather offered by the dawn had been splendidly fulfilled, for the air was clear as starlight and felt fresh and clean, as though the recent rain had purged it of all impurities. Far away north the sea shone like a thin blue line. Roads and fields, made small by distance, though not obscured, maintained their sharpness of outline mile after mile, until they met the coast. Like chips on the edge of china bowl were the river mouths. Although the horizon was so clear along the sea, billowy masses of cream-coloured clouds floated ponderously in the east. And the shadows of the clouds lay sombre and blue on the lines. As they climbed flying north, Warton noticed the ground slipping diagonally away towards the left. 'Strong west wind,' he thought, and decided to bear the fact in mind. He amused himself getting close up to one or other of the flanking machines. Mellor looked up and waved a hand at him, while his observer, Dodge, who was practising rifle exercises with the spare joy-stick, presented arms. When he approached Savage's machine, Ryeward swung his gun round and took aim with such a business-like manner, that he swerved instinctively away. Ryeward noticed the movement, and signified contempt by expressive gestures.

Meanwhile, the formation had very nearly reached the coast, and Warton was struck by the toy-like appearance of the little ships that crawled over the water with scarcely perceptible motion. A small port lay beneath them resembling a spider with its two jetties curving out into the channel. A ragged fringe of white edged the jetties, and the waters beyond were wrinkled and opaque, but inside the harbour they lay flawless and opalescent like thin blown glass.

Beyond the belt of sea England's coast marked the horizon by a line narrow and green.

When they turned inland once more, Warton looked back over his shoulder and thought whimsically that twenty minutes' flight would carry him to his home. They had now reached a height of 12,000 feet, but Fories wished to climb considerably higher before crossing the lines, lest Huns should be lurking in the glare of the sun. By the time they reached their own section of the front once more, an hour had elapsed, and 15,000 feet separated them from the earth. Warton realised suddenly that he was cold; bitterly cold. His fingers were stinging and throbbing under the heavy gauntlet that he wore, and every time he looked along the cowling the wind seared his cheeks till they felt as though the skin were being stripped from them. As he breathed, the wind-screen became coated with an ever-thickening film of ice. He beat his finger-tips against the instrument board, but the pain they caused him was so intense, that he desisted hastily, and resigned himself to frostbite. The hands of his watch seemed to remain stationary. He judged an interval of ten minutes to discover that they had only registered three. Then he tried to fix his mind on other subjects. He watched Savage, and hoped he was feeling cold also. Surely that ass Fories would turn for the lines now and get the show done! Archie, Huns, anything was better than this gnawing cold. He wished to heaven that he had put on another pair of gloves, or that his engine would fail and compel him to land somewhere where he could get warm. But the rev.-indicator remained steady, so he decided to kill the first Hun that put in an appearance instead.

'I'll shoot the beggar down in flames,' he thought. 'Gad, though! If he's anything like as cold as I am, it would be a pleasure for him!'

Meanwhile, Fories had been anxiously scrutinising the east for signs of an enemy. Not a black speck anywhere could be seen above the impassive clouds. He turned to the left, and after five minutes the lines were behind them. Warton was amazed at the tremendous depths of the clouds. They seemed to be piled on top of one another in gigantic pyramids, 10,000 feet from apex to base. Dazzlingly white they were at the summits, and their walls were daubed with buff and gray, that merged together into sepia down on the lower strata. Where one cloud threw its shadow across another, there appeared a dark blue fan, azure tipped. Looking downwards to the floor of the valleys, he caught glimpses of devastated country. Although he would have been the last to admit it, Warton had a keen sense of beauty, and the majesty of this scenery so impressed him, that all thoughts of war were driven from his mind, and he even forgot the cold. He was brought to his senses by a sharp crack that bespoke the activity of Archie batteries below. Fories led his formation round a towering edifice of vapour, and the Archie bursts were left behind, looking like stains of watery drawing-ink on a sheet of blue paper.

It was then that Warton realised the possibilities afforded by these clouds. Like fighting in close country, one never knew but that the enemy might be just out of sight, yet close at *hand*. He felt as though they were playing a game of hide-and-seek, and every time they turned to explore a new gulf, he strained forward and glanced expectantly over the top plane and under the wings. Once he caught sight of a white machine thousands of feet below, that was shining like a minnow in the sun. He pointed it out to Lastor and yelled 'Hun!' at the top of his voice. Lastor nodded, and fired a few rounds at the distant target. Warton watched the red streaks of tracer swerve downwards and vanish before he turned to test his own gun. There was a short, sharp rattle, and then silence. He glanced at the crank-handle. 'Number one!' he grunted. 'Gun cold! Just like me!' He warmed it up with a few more bursts, looked round the cockpit at his taps and instruments, and then fixed his eyes once more on Fories.

The leader was turning round the circumference of a large circle, and examining a column of clear air that pierced the clouds like a mineshaft. This gap was perhaps a mile in diameter at the top, but it appeared to narrow funnelwise towards the ground, which was hazy and blue. Three times Fories flew round the mouth of the funnel, with his followers crossing over from side to side so as to keep formation. And looking down, Warton saw the Huns. Almost invisible against the earth, first one then another would flash into sight and remain silhouetted for a second against the white wall of cloud, before dropping back into the mist. He counted up to six and then abandoned the task for it was impossible to follow the movements of each individual. Like a school of porpoises, they appeared to be playing round each other, diving, turning, and banking. Fories decided to attack.

Having shut off his engine, he was obliged to spiral down owing to the proximity of the cloud walls. Warton, with heart beating fast, crouched forward in his seat, pulled up the handle of the synchronised gear, glanced through his sight to make sure that the lenses were clean, and edged in close between Savage and Mellor. Standing up in the back, Lastor swung his gun-mounting about, and tested the magazine on its post. From a thousand feet, Warton saw that the enemy were fat-bellied scouts, painted cream, pale green, and buff, or mottled azure and brown. Their top planes were longer than the bottom; their bodies were round and gleaming; and they had tails like a fish. Then Fories dived and got behind a German machine that wriggled and swerved like a salmon pursued by an otter, before it dropped to earth with thick black smoke pouring from its fuselage. Warton just saw the conclusion of this opening duel, as Lastor's gun rattled and a cream-coloured body with muddy wings flashed overhead, so close that the wheels of its undercarriage seemed almost within reach. As he noticed its thin black crosses, the machine dived down straight into his gun-sight. Exultantly he pushed the throttle open and followed. Only twenty yards separated him from the German, and it seemed as though at such range bullets could not miss. He could see the pilot's helmeted head and the greasy breath from the engine's exhaust. Every wire of the machine stood out sharp and clear in the lens of his sight; his gun chattered and smoked unceasingly, but the Hun never burst into flames as he expected. Instead, the machine turned swiftly over on to its back. There was a glimpse of a shining round body, and the two little struts of an undercarriage, as it fell away and to one side under the left wing.

Perhaps the pilot had been hit, but before Warton could follow his dive, Lastor gripped him by the shoulder and pointed upwards. A mass of fire and smoke was falling towards them. Emerging from the flames behind was the dark green fin and coloured rudder of a British machine. When he realised that fact, Warton forgot all else. He kept his eyes fixed on the blazing wreckage, unconsciously diving to keep pace with its fall. It seemed to be poised almost stationary in the air, like a barbed spear-head whose haft was smoke. As they approached, Warton could dimly recognise the forms of planes protruding from an envelope of rippling fire. Wing tips and tail alone were visible, for the body seemed wrapped in scarlet tatters. Suddenly, appearing as it were from the heart of the furnace, a human figure stood up. Black and terrible, it remained motionless for the fraction of a second before being caught by the wind and hurled lurchingly away. Light flashed momentarily on a leather coat and muffled face. Then, falling arm over arm, the body dwindled to a speck and vanished. Lastor was banging his pilot on the arm and shrieking, 'Triplanes! Man alive! Triplanes!' Warton jerked the stick back into his stomach, and when next he looked, there was nothing but a plume of smoke that trailed from an ashen shell.

From all directions the triplanes attacked them. Little vicious machines they were, painted in chequers, scarlet and gold, black, white, and yellow. Their polished cowlings gleamed; and as they banked the fabric tautened glittering along the camber-ribs. Bullets crackled through the wings and splintered the woodwork. A flying wire twanged as it snapped; the compass above Warton's head burst and sprinkled him with water. Everywhere the air was traversed by the thick blue lines of smoke tracer. Little red bullets streamed past between the planes over the centre section, from under the tail. Desperately Warton turned and swung in his efforts to escape; at every point he was met by three planes, and whirling propeller blades. At his back, Lastor was standing up, and firing coolly as each target presented itself. One of his tracer bullets hit a Hun petrol tank and the machine dived vertically, burning fiercely. Another staggered, side-slipped, and spun, with a dead pilot gripping the controls. Yet ever their numbers seemed to increase.

Warton glanced at his altimeter; only eight thousand feet;–he dare not lose any more height. Yet the clouds offered shelter. Instinctively he turned and flew straight for a few seconds, but he was pulled round by Lastor, who foresaw the withering fire that would be poured upon them. 'By God!' thought Warton, 'if I go down one of these brutes is going with me!' He turned and made for a triplane slightly below him. Heedless of passing bullets he kept the machine in his gun-sight, following its every movement, firing the while. The Hun's top wing buckled, and all three planes tore themselves apart. 'One down!' said Warton to himself as he kicked the rudder bar, and brought his gun on to a fresh target. This time a flash of flame burst from behind the pilot's seat. 'Two down!' he continued. 'Now, where are the rest?' Before that question could be answered, sky, Huns, everything, was obliterated by thick vapour. They had reached the wall of clouds.

Never had Warton imagined that the damp gray interior of a cloud could afford him such comfort. Rejoicing to think that they were invisible, he sat back in his seat, and wiped the moisture from his forehead, wondering whether it were sweat or condensed mist. Two Huns, he had shot down; Lastor another two. That was not so bad for one machine. Then he remembered that one of his companions had gone down in flames. Quickly he throttled back, and shouted at his observer. 'Who was it that went down? No, I didn't say we nearly went down. I said, who was it went down in flames?'

'Oh! Mellor or Fories, I think. I saw one streamer, but couldn't be sure of two. Mellor, probably,' answered Lastor.

'Sure it wasn't Savage?'

'Yes. Quite sure. But Lord knows where the others have got to. I say! Do you know the petrol tank's been shot through? No! Not the Hun's, you silly ass! Ours! Our–rear–petrol–tank–has–been–shot. Got that?'

'No! Has it really? We'd better be getting back west. There's not too much petrol left in the front tank. Which way is west? The compass has been smashed.'

'Try and climb to an open space and find the sun. Turn a bit to the left. There! That's enough. I think we're about right now.'

For a few minutes they flew as straight as was possible, Warton keeping his eyes fixed on the speed indicator and bubble. Then he shut off the engine again.

'Hi! Lastor!' he yelled. 'Wasn't it a hell of a fight? I saw your two Huns. Did you see mine? Are you sure it wasn't Savage?'

'Yes, man! I saw. No, it wasn't. Stop talking until we're out of this mess. We're miles over the lines still!'

After a few minutes' flight they emerged into a valley of clear air, and discovered from the sun that their direction had been very nearly due north. For some distance the gap between the clouds ran due east and west, and away on their left side, Warton recognised a big triangular forest and the straight canal that led home. Then the engine spluttered, and the rev.-indicator needle swung violently to and fro. 'Lord help us!' thought Warton. 'What the devil's wrong now?' While waiting for his engine to stop completely, with his eye he measured the distance that lay between them and the lines. They might just be able to do it, though the strong west wind was fighting against them.

Yet still spluttering and banging, the engine continued its work, as though striving desperately to get them home. Losing height steadily they headed for the lines! Never before had the ground seemed to crawl so slowly past. Warton turned taps on and off; pumped up pressure, glanced at his oil gauge; tried every expedient that he could think of. Nowhere could he find anything wrong. 'Must be ignition!' he concluded, and fixed his eyes once more on the slowly approaching lines. Two thousand feet high, three miles to go; and the wind dead against them. 'Lastor,' he yelled over his shoulder, 'sorry, old man.

Afraid we shan't do it. You'd better look out for a crash.' Then he noticed that Lastor was standing up, waving his arms excitedly, and shouting. An Archie battery immediately below opened on them; machine-gun tracers fired from the ground leapt past. Warton leant back and signalled to his observer to shout in his ear.

'Vacuum!' bellowed Lastor. 'Have you shut your vacuum control?' He glanced at the lever. It was open. And as he closed it the engine roared with renewed life.

Fifteen minutes later, his machine bumped to a standstill on the tarmac. Fories broke away from a group of officers and ran over to meet him. 'Where the blazes have you been?' he asked speaking rapidly. 'Damn good show! I saw your Huns. Poor old Mellor went down. Lost sight of you, and thought you were killed. We ran into the Circus, and Savage and I got away together. How many did you swipe? Four? Good enough! That makes ten altogether. Gad! You have been shot about. Rotten luck about Mellor. 'Strewth! What a scrap!'

There seemed to be crowds of men round Warton, who all talked together and congratulated him. Their presence brought back to his mind the vision of Mellor's machine flaming and falling. Swaying a little, he caught hold of a strut and was violently sick.

Chapter VI

Spring Offensive

'With a hey-ney-ninny-nonny-no,' sang Lastor blithely, sitting up in bed, and beating time with a cane against the wall of the hut. 'Do you realise, Longeron, old bean,' he continued, addressing Warton, 'that to-day is a perfectly good squadron holiday?'

Warton opened one eye, and glared sternly at him over the top of his blankets. 'There's no need to make such a filthy row even if it is,' he answered. 'Oh! For Lord's sake, sing another tune. You're giving the dog a fit.' Blackie, the terrier, who had been sleeping at the foot of Savage's bed, felt impelled to deny this accusation by a furious burst of barking. Savage sprang out of bed and chased Blackie round the hut with a broom. A bundle of blankets in Ryeward's corner stirred uneasily and moaned.

'Jove!' said Warton, as he stumbled his way to the window. 'Isn't it good to think we shan't be compelled to aviate to-day? Jolly fine day, too! Are you coming into town, Savage?'

'Perhaps hardly to town; still, to the gay little coastal village of Boulogne all the same.' replied Savage. 'In other words–I'm on!'

'Lastor's coming, of course,' continued Warton. 'But how about that thing in the corner he said, pointing to Ryeward's muffled form.

'Oh! That!' returned Savage, with a contemptuous sniff. 'It's not coming with me! I don't like being seen in public with an observer who fires Very lights into the cockpit!'

'It wasn't the cockpit!' yelled Ryeward, shooting his head suddenly up from under the blankets. 'It was the—'

'That's quite enough,' said Savage, holding up a silencing hand. 'We won't discuss the disgraceful episode further. If you promise to behave, we'll allow you to go to Boulogne with us.'

'Go to Boulogne yourself!' Ryeward bellowed, thoroughly roused. 'It's the kind of filthy little hole you'd care for.' He buried his head under the blankets again, and growled in a muffled voice. 'Go to blazes! I'm not going!'

'What a sweet temper our little friend is in this morning!' murmured Savage. With the exception of Ryeward the inmates of the hut set about making preparations for the day. Kit-bags were ransacked in search for appropriate garments. The batman was burdened with field boots and injunctions to excel himself. A long and searching argument raged between Warton and his observer as to whether slacks or riding breeches would be more fitting to the occasion.

When all preparations had been completed, and the party was waiting outside the mess for the tender that was to convey them to Boulogne, Ryeward, in a half-dressed and very dishevelled condition, rushed out of the hut shouting, 'Hi, there! Can't you people wait five minutes while a fellow finishes dressing?' Still muttering incoherently, he disappeared and slammed the door.

Savage groaned. 'The only excuse one could make for Ryeward,' he said, 'is that he suffers from an artistic temperament. And that is less of an excuse than an apology.' However, simultaneously with the appearance of the tender, Ryeward emerged, buckling on his Sam Browne, and calling on heaven to witness that Savage had stolen his cane. When that dispute had been adjusted, and the uproar inside the tender, due to there being at least two candidates for every seat, had subsided, they departed. The major, as he watched them go laughing and shouting down the road, smiled to himself; then returned to his book and his parrot. Three weeks had elapsed since the fight in which Mellor had lost his life, and the squadron had averaged two patrols a day throughout that time. Although they had suffered no further casualties, the major was glad of the rest afforded to his pilots by this holiday.

Warton and Savage had secured the two seats next to the driver, and so were able to enjoy the sparkling sunshine and the wind that seemed to anticipate the coming of spring. Women worked in the fields, and occasionally they passed a small child driving a wagon, or a herd of cattle, but otherwise they did not meet a soul. Over on a hillside to the east they saw a black patch of charred grass and wood that marked the last landing place of a night raider. Floating low over the tree-tops was the observation balloon whence Meteor surveyed the heavens and issued his prophecies.

An hour's drive brought them to the outskirts of Boulogne, through which they crawled, impeded by street urchins and tram lines. They stopped outside the officers' club, and the party, having made arrangements to reassemble there at ten o'clock in the evening, dispersed in twos and threes.

Shortly after, Warton, Savage, and their observers were sitting on a bench facing the sea, watching the crowd of Tommies, French soldiers, and civilians that passed up and down. 'What an enormous number of girls there are in the world!' said Savage. 'Look at 'em all! Short ones, tall ones, fat ones, thin ones; all animated by the same desire–to catch the eye of some man with enough money to keep them amused!'

'Yes,' chimed in Ryeward, 'and look at all the men, whiskered and unwhiskered, whose one object in life is to attract the attention of the aforesaid girls!'

'You are right,' answered Savage. 'There are many fools in the world; and still not enough to go round.'

'Oh, rot to you and your cynicism!' Ryeward cried. 'I'm sure you are always reading sentimental enough books.'

'That's just the point,' said Savage. 'Sentiment is all very well in literature. But feminine charm depends on the absence of women.'

Ryeward's reply consisted of a snort.

They spent the afternoon wandering through the streets buying odds and ends that they did not want, and in the evening took a ramshackle old cab, and drove out to Wimereux. The veteran horse broke down on the hill and the driver nearly came to blows with Warton, who called him *cochon* instead of *cocher*. After this incident, they went to a restaurant for dinner and throughout the whole meal discussed flying, and their careers after the war.

'If they'll have me,' said Warton, 'I'll keep on flying after the war. There's nothing else for me to do. I don't know anything.'

'The day peace is declared,' rejoined Lastor, 'I intend to start an exhaustive study of the art of assassination, so as to be able to administer justice to those who still insist on talking shop. What are your plans, Savage?'

'Like Warton, I'll stay in if it's possible,' said Savage. 'The intellectual side of military matters rather appeals to me. I shall get my sister to sew a red band on my straw-hat, and sit in an office devising new army forms. In the course of time, a grateful nation will present me with a piece of ribbon worth one-three-farthings a yard. And when I've saved a couple of hundred pounds, I'll buy myself a title or a Ford car. Now it's your turn, Ryeward.'

'Oh! I'll chuck flying, and take up farming.'

'On second thoughts,' said Savage meditatively, 'I think I'll become a professional democrat. It's so profitable. Democracy consists of sharing venison with an earl, and keeping your bag of winkles to yourself. It enables one to approach even taxi-drivers with an air of equality.'

At that moment a young man wearing three very new stars walked out, and trod on Savage's foot as he passed. 'Why the 'ell don't yer keep yer feet to yerself,' he growled.

'The higher, the fewer!' replied Savage, smiling sweetly. 'Now that provides a very fine example of the distinction between a temporary officer and a temporary gentleman,' he continued, regarding the captain's retreating back. 'To the former promotion means an increase in his responsibilities; to the latter, an increase in the number of people he can be rude to.'

At ten o'clock they went round to the post office and met the tender. After waiting some time for two stragglers, they set out and jolted silent and sleepy on their way back to the camp. The major was sitting in the mess ruffling the parrot's feathers with his forefinger as they entered.

'Hallo, chaps!' he said. 'Have a good time? You'll all have to pack up your kits to-morrow. We're going to shunt to an aerodrome down south the next day. Looks as though there's going to be trouble down there.'

Wearily Savage leant on Warton's shoulder while they walked over to the hut. 'Strafe these moves!' he groaned. 'Just as we get comfortable at one place, they boost us off to a new one. Half the kit will get lost on the way. There are probably no huts at this place, and we shall have to live in tents up to our eyebrows in mud. Nobody knows the lines down there. Oh, Lord!'

'I've never met such a wrinkled and miserable grouser as you in all my natural,' answered Warton. 'I think the change will be rather interesting.'

'Alas for the elasticity of youth!' continued Savage in the same mournful monotone.

'Shut up!' Ryeward exclaimed impatiently. 'When you aren't trying to be funny or clever, you're howling over some misery or other!'

In silence the quartet undressed and went to bed.

Fortunately the next day was so rainy that flying was out of the question, and so they were able to devote their whole attention to packing. Ryeward, of course, refused to move a finger in the matter, for he claimed that all his kit could be packed in ten minutes. Throughout the day, therefore, he sat on his bed smoking and passing scornful remarks on his companions.

The next morning, in spite of the heavy mist, all the machines left the ground, and, led by their flight commanders, flew in formations of four or five towards the south. Into the back seat of his machine, Warton had wedged a couple of suitcases and a number of canes and caps, so that Lastor experienced considerable difficulty in getting into his seat at all. The ground was covered by a blanket of thick white mist, about fifty feet thick. Sticking out of the mist like rocks from the sea were church steeples, the tops of tall trees, and, here and there, the conical-shaped slag-heaps of a coal-mine. Away to the east the sun shone through thin horizontal streaks of cloud, in alternate layers of slate and orange.

Warton, as he listened to the wailing wires and the steady smooth voice of his engine, felt invincibly superior to any German machines in the air. He looked round his cockpit and noted with pride the clean polish of the dashboard set with black instrument dials; the blue metallic glint on the crank handle of his gun; and the rough yellow brass of the synchronised gear handle, that was shining in a little patch of sunlight.

His breath, freezing on the wind-screen, traced patterns with spiral fans and bristling shafts of ice that caught the light along their ribs and edges. Singing softly to himself, he cleared the frosted wind-screen with the finger of his gauntlet. Then he turned round and shouted at Lastor, whose face, blue with cold, peered at him over the luggage. 'By Jove!' he said, 'isn't it a topping morning?'

'Yes, beastly!' returned Lastor through his chattering teeth.

By this time the ground mist had cleared away, and he saw that they were following a straight road that disappeared into the southern horizon. At intervals all along the road were little black caterpillars that he knew to be bodies of men, marching. Long convoys of lorries there were also, and gun trains and horses. Even the side roads were black with movement. In a hollow by the side of the road he saw a number of pale green objects, each one thrown into sharp relief by a diamond-shaped shadow. The mud about them was traversed in every direction by broad-ribbed tracks.

'Tanks!' he yelled, and pointed them out to Lastor. Farther on the ground was broken by gravel mounds and quarries speckled with dark vegetation. On the patches of grass between the quarries were line upon line of horses, and an ant-like activity of many hundreds of men. Away to the east was the muddy yellow strip of no-man's-land, and behind the strip ran a castellated system of trenches in gray and ochre, linking up with each other like an immense Greek key pattern. Above his head, Warton noticed a formation of fifteen scouts, shining in the sun, and farther west were still more machines. Infantry, artillery, machines, all were moving south. They passed over a town sprawling between the ploughed land and the river marshes. Like a hollow tooth, the roofless cathedral, surrounded by its ulcerated ruins, looked as though it must experience pain to be thus exposed in the bitter morning air. Shadows on the river appeared of a softer blue by contrast with its shining belts of silver. Between the many branches of the waterways lay islands faintly green. Warton thought that they would make ideal mooring-places for a punt during the warm hours of a summer's afternoon. With speculative eyes he watched a bursting shell throw up its foul smudge of smoke and dust. From the town they followed another road that led south-west, and, twenty minutes later, a white light falling like a star from the leader's machine told of their journey's end. Warton was not at all favourably impressed by the appearance of the aerodrome from above. The main road ran across it between the hangars, and to the west of the road the ground appeared to slope down towards a small stream, while to the east it was shut in by a wood. He waited until all the other machines had landed and crawled up to the sheds, then he flew low over the tree-tops, side-slipped away his height, and floated up-wind along the grass. When he heard the tail skid grate, he sighed with relief.

Leaving his machine in charge of the mechanics who had been sent over by lorry the preceding night, Warton joined the group of pilots and observers who were strolling across the aerodrome towards the officers' quarters. They were all relieved to find that Nissen huts had been provided for them, and that the mess was in good repair. Savage had already staked out claims in a hut for his three friends, and with his helmet pushed back from his forehead and a pipe stuck between his teeth, was industriously sweeping the floor with a number of rags tied to the end of a pole. 'Hallo, youngsters!' he said as they entered. 'Wipe your feet and then say a prayer over our domestic hearth. Godliness is next to cleanliness!'

Having piled his flying clothes in a corner, Warton sat down and fumbled for a cigarette. The exultation in flying that had filled him that morning had passed, and he now felt very tired. Through a tear in the window fabric, a thin ray of sunlight entered, throwing a vivid spark on the muddy boards. Framed in by the doorway, he noticed a hedgerow sprinkled with pale green buds. An incessant rumbling and splashing on the road outside came from the passing lorries.

He got up and threw his cigarette away. 'Damn this blasted idiotic war!' he muttered. 'Give me some tobacco someone. I want a pipe.'

Savage looked at him with a smile, leaning on his broom-pole. 'I know that feeling,' he said. 'It always comes in the spring.' He produced a tobacco pouch and a book. 'Try both,' he suggested. 'Tobacco and its twin sister, literature.' Warton glanced at the title of the book.

'*The Book of Artemas*,' he said, 'sounds familiar.' Five minutes later he laughed long and loud.

'Infallible!' murmured Savage.

By this time the other two flights had arrived, and a sound of banging doors and tramping feet, together with much argument, marked their choice of quarters. Fories looked in at the door for a moment.

'Hallo, you people!' he said. 'Are you all O.K. in here? There's no grub arrived yet, so we've arranged to go in flights to a pub just down the road. We shall be going at twelve. Show this afternoon. Leave ground at 2.30.'

'Right-o!' returned Warton, and settled down again to his book.

The 'pub' of which Fories had spoken turned out to be an incredibly dirty and very smelly farm-house, built round a quadrangle. Dirty straw and manure littered the uneven cobbles of the courtyard, which contained in its centre a small pond whose surface was coated with green scum. The plaster was peeling from the walls, and the moss-speckled roof with its broken back seemed on the point of collapse. Warton, turning into a doorway which he imagined was the entrance, encountered the mildly inquiring gaze of a cow. He apologised and went on. In spite of its unprepossessing exterior, the house inside was clean and well kept. They were shown into the kitchen, where red tiles on the floor jumped as they were trodden on. Over a stove in the corner there stooped an old woman engaged in preparing an omelette. Kitchen utensils stood on shelves of coarse, unplaned wood; jugs were suspended from nails. Round one angle of the room ran a bench, blackened and polished by the repose of many generations. Three chairs and the table completed the furniture. Ornaments there were none, save a copy of the restrictions on alcohol that, in a curled and mildewed condition, flapped above the door. The old woman appeared to live there alone, with two small urchins, whose mouths bore signs of a recent meal. She provided her guests with a Gargantuan omelette, segments from a long cylindrical loaf, butter, and coffee. Having eaten all that was offered, 'A' flight made room for its successors, and returned to the aerodrome.

They left the ground at 2.30 that afternoon. Isolated clouds drifted over from the west, where a bluish-gray mist indicated the advent of rain. Gun flashes sparkled incessantly along the lines, and the ground was dotted with puffs of smoke, whose shapes stood hard and definite for a few brief seconds ere they were scattered slowly by the wind. Barely fifteen minutes had elapsed before Warton had completely lost his bearings. This unfamiliar country seemed to offer no landmarks such as he had been accustomed to. Small woods and fields succeeded one another monotonously; the roads twisted as they followed the contours, and the villages were as alike as houses in a suburban road. In the south-east, shining dimly through the haze like golden scales, he could see patches of water and the vast shadow of a town. Fories crossed the lines at five thousand feet, still below the level of the clouds, but he did not go far over. On this patrol he was more concerned with learning the country than fighting. A few artillery machines going about their lawful business patrolled the lines, and far away east in the sunlight were six Huns playing above their aerodrome. It seemed to Warton as though the land were waiting in hushed expectancy for the bursting of a storm. As the gray light of rain crept towards them, gun flashes stood out more vividly, and the smoke of blasting shells glowed fitfully against its background. Lastor leant forward and tapped his pilot on the arm as a signal for him to throttle back.

'Hell of a war on!' he yelled. 'Spring offensive. Look at all the Hun junk on those roads!' Warton nodded, and turned his attention again to Fories. For some time past Archie had been worrying them, but now of a sudden it had ceased. The silence was ominous. To the leader's mind it could have but one interpretation–Huns! Out of sight behind a cloud, but visible from the ground he knew there must be a hostile formation. Five hundred feet above his head appeared an isolated Archie burst. So that was the signal. He fired a red light to warn his followers, and flew straight waiting for the attack. Down across the flanks of vapour came eight scouts in a scattered, ill-disciplined mob.

As he saw their three planes and petal-shaped rudders, Fories muttered under his breath, 'Damn! These blasted little tripes again!' With the first blue streaks of tracer he turned sharply east so as to gain protection from the Germans' wings. The leading triplane dived steeper and steeper in an endeavour to keep a sight on Fories, and finally swooped straight through the British formation, unable to check its enormous speed. It was pursued by a flashing stream of bullets from the observer's gun. Warton glanced over the side at the little patch of burning wreckage among the shell holes, and was met by a stinging blast of raindrops. In a few seconds his goggles and wind-screen were opaque from the water that filled the air, and blotted out the ground. Water swept past in swinging curtains like some gray Aurora Borealis; muffled the engine's roar with its surge and rattle; confused earth and sky together; and hurled the machine from side to side, with its atmospheric eddies. When he pushed up his useless goggles Warton was blinded as though an acid had been flung in his eyes. The compass refused guidance by spinning madly round on its pivot; the bubble rushed frenziedly from one side of its arc to the other; and all the instruments seemed to be dancing behind their streaming dials of glass. Gusts of wind rocked the machine by hammer-like blows under the wings, now lifting it bodily into the air, now causing it to drop like a stone. Warton felt sick, giddy, half paralysed. He crouched forward in his seat, cleared the face of the air-speed indicator, and endeavoured to fix its wavering needle at seventy. Then he pushed the throttle lever fully forward, opened the radiator blind, and concentrated all his energies on climbing above the storm. There followed a period of hideous discomfort, during which the controls jumped under his hand as though possessed of devils, while the drenching rain sought out all the crevices in his clothing and chilled him to the bone. Gradually the colour of the mist above them lightened, changing from gray to white, until a few ragged patches of blue showed that the ceiling had been reached. As they soared out between two shining turrets of vapour into the upper reaches, Warton was struck by the awe-inspiring silence that seemed so absolute after the turmoil they had passed through. Steady, save for the slight quivering of the wings, they climbed towards the sun and surveyed the calm expanse of cloud which extended in all directions to the horizon, billow after billow, like a snowy sea. Warton looked over his shoulder and grinned at Lastor who was sitting huddled up and almost sunk below the clotted fur collar of his coat.

'Any idea where we are?' he shouted.

'Don't be funny, but fly west,' came the answer.

The compass, recovered from its attack of spinning, had jammed itself immovably in a tilted position, so Warton judged his direction by keeping the sun on his left front. He calculated that half an hour's flight would bring him a long way west of the lines, and it was then his intention to descend through the clouds and search for a landmark or an aerodrome. Towards the west the cloud valleys became darker and greener, suggesting earth below. At first vague, then slowly acquiring definition, roads appeared through the mist, while here and there a clear rift enclosed some fleeting glimpse of town or wood. Through one of these rifts Warton caught sight of a row of hangars gleaming in a passing shaft of sunlight. He flew round in a circle studying the little patch of ground. Lastor was standing up, leaning over his shoulder, and staring at him with an inquiring gaze.

'Well! How about it?' said Warton.

'Looks to me like a perfectly good aerodrome,' answered his observer.

'Are you sure it isn't Hun?'

Lastor nodded doubtfully. 'Don't think so. Go down and have a look.'

'Yes, but supposing it is Hun!'

'Then nip back quick into the clouds.'

Warton shrugged his shoulders and commenced to spiral down. On emerging below the storm wrack he felt the tingling raindrops striking his face again, and his goggles became so blurred that he almost lost sight of the aerodrome. Instinctively he judged the direction of the wind, and glided down so as to cross the road very low and land near the hangars. When about fifty feet above the ground, he pushed his goggles up and glanced over the side. Close by the sheds was a cream-coloured aeroplane, whose stripped wings lay alongside the fuselage. Two black crosses on the planes stared ominously at him. A body of men in gray uniforms were marching down the road. He could see their pink faces as they looked up and watched him pass. With a shock that seemed to spread from his heart outwards, he recognised machine and men as Huns. Instantly his hand jumped to the throttle lever, and the engine deepened its note. Yet not as before was the sound it made, but mingled with strange snorts and groans. Barely able to keep in the air, his machine floated for several hundred yards across the grass. Then with a final explosive wheeze the engine gave out completely, and the aeroplane dropped silently and heavily on to the ground.

Half blinded by the rain, Warton yelled to his observer. 'This is a blasted Hun aerodrome, and the engine's cold! Get out and give her suck-in. For God's sake buck up!'

Lastor was already in front heaving at the reluctant propeller with all his weight. Glancing over towards the half obscured hangars, Warton saw two tiny human figures that ran through the rain towards him. Panting, and with water streaming from his face, Lastor stood back as he twirled the self-starter handle. A snort and a convulsive twitch came from the engine; then silence again.

'Try her once more. She'll go next time! Oh, Lord! The damn radiator's jammed! 'Strewth! No pressure! Oh, hell! Here come the Huns! All clear! Contact!'

The engine gave another sullen bellow and then stopped dead.

'It's no use!' said Lastor, running round to his seat. 'I'll get a Very light and blow the brute up.' He disappeared below the gun-mounting, and a sound of scuffling ensued mingled with interjections. 'Phew! The rack's gone. All the lights are half-way down the fuselage. Spilt all over the place. Ugh!'

Warton stared dully at the dirty grass, with blind fury filling his mind. To be taken prisoner had been an abiding fear with him ever since he left England. Arrogant Huns; months in a prison camp; barbed wire; black bread; the hideous future unrolled itself before him like a panorama. Abruptly he jumped out and leant against the wing, listening to the thumping feet of the approaching Huns, and to Lastor as he strove to reach a Very light. He was awakened from his reverie by hearing a respectful voice inquire:

'Will you give her suck-in, please, sir?'

'Uncomprehendingly he stared at the figure who was grasping the propeller. Its features were hidden by the blade, but of the rest there could be no doubt that it wore a khaki uniform. Warton glanced round the aerodrome, but gained nothing thereby, for all landmarks were enveloped in rain and mist.

'What squadron is there on this aerodrome?' he asked, turning towards the khaki figure; then paused as he recognised the face of his fitter-corporal, who was staring at him with an expression of blank astonishment. For a brief second, Warton gazed at the man silently before bursting into a wild peal of laughter. He was still leaning up against the fuselage, laughing helplessly, when Lastor appeared, standing up in the cockpit, very red in the face, and grasping a loaded Very pistol.

When they had taxied the machine over to the sheds, they went to inspect the German machine that had caused so much anxiety. Batches of German prisoners were still marching sullenly past down the road, under the escort of small but ferocious Tommies.

'No wonder we thought this was Hun-land, with all those nightmares walking about!' said Lastor.

Standing by the Albatross was the flight sergeant. He saluted as Warton came up.

'You're the only one who's got back so far, sir, except Captain Fories,' he said. 'Not a bad machine this. Belongs to a Naval Squadron who came here this afternoon.'

'Does it?' returned Warton, with a note of irritation in his voice. 'Well, I wish they wouldn't leave their debris lying about all over the place.'

The flight sergeant grinned, and the grin widened until its extent was positively painful to see. 'Excuse me, sir,' he ventured. 'But I saw you try to take off again. Did you mistake this place for a Hun 'drome in the rain an' all?'

Warton flushed very red, and started to move away. 'You'd better have a look at my undercarriage, flight,' he said. 'I think the V-strut's gone a bit.'

'Shrewd fellow, that flight sergeant!' Lastor remarked as they plodded over to the mess.

'Shrewd! I should think he jolly well is!' muttered Warton.

Ground Strafing

Under normal conditions the squadron society was divided roughly into two classes–those who played cards and those who did not. The latter class in turn consisted of a number of small cliques and combinations. There were, for instance, the Heavenly Twins, who played ping-pong all day and half the night; the Moper, who sat pondering darkly for hours over a book whose title he carefully concealed from the public; the Sports Enthusiast, who panted round the camp every morning at dawn in a pair of running shorts; and, finally, the Quartet. Warton, Savage, Lastor, and Ryeward constituted the Quartet. They kept very much to themselves, each passing the time according to his tastes. Warton used to amuse himself in the squadron office, studying types of German machines and planning methods of attack with a pencil and paper; Savage was occupied playing with his terrier Blackie, and learning, so he declared, philosophy from him; Lastor spent most of his time reading English and French poetry; while Ryeward smoked all day and said nothing.

But the period immediately following their move down south saw the squadron united in a common state of anxiety and interest.

Rumours of desperate fighting and an overpowering German offensive were on every man's lips. The mess was full with groups who talked excitedly and discussed the war news. Now it was that the Germans had advanced ten miles, and that every man, gun, and beast was being hurried up to stop them; now that they were being decoyed by a skilful retreat into a trap that was to end the war. Every day some strange machine landed with tales of aerodromes shelled to pieces and captured by the Huns; of kit and even personnel that had had to be abandoned; of fearful odds that were being hurled against the British lines; of confusion, lack of communication; heroic counter attacks that failed to stem the advance; loss of men, guns spiked and left for the enemy; machines burnt.

But, serious as the affair appeared to be, no man was depressed or pessimistic. They seemed rather to regard it all in the light of a huge joke. They would speculate as to their chances of defending the aerodrome with machine-guns and revolvers. The Moper was recommended to stand on guard every night, for it was said that at the sight of him the Huns would burst into tears and run away. Yet, underlying all this levity, there was a very real feeling of anxiety. 'A joke's a joke,' said Savage, 'but this is a calamity!'

The major, who probably knew more how matters stood than any one else, was loud in his assertion that the Huns were being allowed to come through so that a large number could be cut off and destroyed. He proved with the aid of a map and a little ingenuity that the end of the war was only a few months ahead.

On the third day after their arrival, came an order for 'Vic' Squadron to proceed for the purpose of trench-strafing and firing on ground targets to a certain strip of country indicated by pin-points. Fories called his flight together in the squadron office and unfurled a map before them. As he laid his finger on the piece of country allotted to them, he whistled and ejaculated, 'Phew! But this is some push! Why the place is only eight miles away! Now, I want you all to fly with me in formation to the picnic ground, and, when I fire a green light, break up into twos and do your damnedest. Warton will come with me; Savage and Barnes go together; Thessinger and Murphy. Be careful not to fire on our troops. Don't go too far over. Don't fly straight. And don't forget to take a toothbrush with you. Leave ground in quarter of an hour's time.'

Lastor was struggling into his flying-coat when Warton entered the hut. 'Now we're in for it good and proper!' he ejaculated between gasps. 'Ever done any trench-strafing? It's a cross between hell fire and an election riot, with an Arctic gale thrown in.' Still groping round his back for the belt of his coat, he slammed the door, and tramped over to the armoury for his gun.

Warton sat down on his bed, and stared unseeingly at the wall opposite. A kind of cold pain was gripping his breast-bone, and when he tried to swallow, his breath escaped hissing between his teeth. He passed his hand uncertainly through his hair. "Strewth!' he muttered. 'I suppose this is what they call wind up!'

Mechanically he rose to his feet, and commenced tugging at his big thigh boots. It seemed as though he were doing everything for the last time, and his mind was filled with one persistent thought–that he was going to be killed. Reason had fled completely, leaving only a black horror and sense of desertion. An air of unreality overhung everything. He regarded the hut, his bed, the tattered pictures, the familiar writing on a letter he had received that day, even himself, with the eyes of an extraneous person seeing these things for the first time.

Then he opened the door, and stood on the threshold, gazing at the little chips of blue sky showing between the twigs of a tree overhead, the while he fumbled clumsily with the scarf about his neck.

A small and quaint figure resembling a golliwog, rushed round the corner of the hut, skidded, and prostrated itself at full length in six inches of mud. It was Barnes, the Canadian. Warton threw back his head and roared with laughter; and, because his laughter rang false in his own ears, therefore he laughed the longer. Barnes, having cursed himself and the mud in round terms, turned and poured his wrathful eloquence on Warton's head. Still laughing, Warton splashed across the road on to the aerodrome. The bad moment had passed. Yet, as he went, he took hold of Barnes's arm, although he was a man for whom he had but little regard.

Within a few moments of leaving the ground, the machines were enveloped in fleeting wisps of vapour. The air felt clammy, wet, and so cold that leather and fur afforded no protection against it. Like shadows on a moving wall of gray, Warton saw his companions as they penetrated deeper into the clouds. Unwilling to risk losing his formation in the mist, Fories dipped, fired a red light to gather them close about him, and flew east at a height of five hundred feet. They passed over little villages, whose cottages showed furtively between the wintry skeletons of trees. Along every road wound an interminable string of lorries, past which there occasionally flashed some furiously-riding motorcyclist. Like graves on the bleak country-side, were the freshly dug trenches. Parties of blue-shirted labourers looked up from their work, attracted by the roaring engines. It was a dreary landscape, painted in sodden grays and dingy yellows.

Warton thrust his chin lower into the face mask he wore, and blew into the soaking fur so as to warm his lips. Never had he felt so uncomfortable in the air. His clothes all seemed to have tied themselves round his neck; one of his shirt sleeves had got screwed up above his elbow, and his forearm was getting thoroughly chilled; his helmet was pinching his ears and ruffling his hair up the wrong way, the strap of his right flying boot had broken, and the boot had slipped down in heavy folds below his knee. To complete his discomfiture, he discovered a good third of an inch play on the joy-stick, and he amused himself rattling the stick about so as to justify his bad temper. These minor irritations had so occupied his mind that the green signal light fired by Fories came as a surprise. He looked over the side, and saw that they had reached the battle-ground. Little yellow puffs of smoke thickly dotted the ground, suddenly appearing and slowly melting away. Occasionally some explosion mightier than the others would throw up red tongues of flame that changed to sullen black smoke. No definite trenches could be seen; only scratches on the earth connecting shell holes. Yet it was but rarely that more than a few yards separated two holes, so closely did they lie together. Dull green water filled their hollows, and round their muddy circumferences lay dark specks, of which some moved and some lay still. A belt of country many miles broad was thus torn and shattered so completely by fire, that almost all landmarks had been obliterated. Here and there, the roofless ruins of a village stared unwinkingly at the sky, or the foundations of some burnt and gutted cottage remained traced like an architect's plan in carbon on brown paper. Splintered and decapitated trunks of trees stood savagely upright in solitude, or herded together bristling on the site of what had once been a wood.

Roads did not exist in this wilderness. They entered from the west; but grew fainter and fainter in outline as they were battered into the surrounding swamps, until they vanished completely. Every visible object was merged into its place in the panorama of war by the slow driving mist.

Warton had obtained a general impression of all these details in the few seconds immediately following the appearance of Fories' green light. The formation broke up into pairs, and Warton found himself following the leader down lower and lower. Two hundred feet was passed by the slow-creeping altimeter needle; then one hundred. As he saw the welter of mud and water rushing past only a few feet below his undercarriage, he murmured: 'Now, God defend me from an engine failure!' He tested each tap; noted with satisfaction the steady needle of his pressure gauge; and pushed the radiator blind full open. The wake of a passing shell shook the machine violently, and made him catch his breath. Dead horses and shapeless bundles of clothes lay scattered in the mud. Some few figures lifted their faces towards him. With relief he noticed they wore khaki. This was the information Fories had been seeking. He rose to five hundred feet again and flew farther east. A stream of tracer bullets that snapped their way through his right wing told him that he had gone far enough. The tail of his machine rose in the air, and he dropped towards the ground. Warton followed, with his engine exerting full power, and the wind screaming and tearing at his face. He saw Fories, like some gigantic bat, flitting in a zig-zag course, so low that he seemed almost to be touching the earth. Spurts of flaming bullets from the back seat told of his observer's activity. Immediately Warton remembered his flight commander's advice– 'don't fly straight.' He kicked hard at the rudder-bar, and the machine skidded outwards and upwards before he steadied it again. A loud report accompanied the appearance of a ball of black smoke just above his head. Instinctively he ducked as some object stuck quivering in the centre section. "Strewth! Archie from field guns!' he thought. The shell holes below were thick with men in gray uniforms. An incessant stream of bullets flashed past him and curved uncertainly upwards into the mist. The air was heavy and agitated by projectiles that hurled the machine about in their passage as though its weight were of no account. Small scouts darted here and there, diving and climbing, worrying the German infantry by their unceasing fire. Ever and again some machine, cut short in its flight, crashed into the ground and flared with a sudden blaze. Many more, like blackened skeletons, burnt fitfully or lay with buckled wings, helplessly on their backs. Dazed from the turmoil, and sweating from the physical exertion of controlling his machine, Warton followed the furious onslaught of his leader, up and down the same belt of shell holes, pouring his fire into the patches of gray as he dived, and listening to the sharp rat-tat-tat-tat of Lastor's gun as they skimmed the ground and climbed again. Time had ceased to exist, and thoughts came slowly to his bewildered brain. For the thousandth time he sang to himself the chorus of a music-hall song, that seemed to blend itself with the Archie bursts, and the explosions on the ground. A scout climbing up across his front tore itself to pieces in a cloud of smoke and fluttered in fragments downwards.

'If you were the only girl in the world!' sang Warton, between his teeth. 'Lord! A direct hit! Poor devil!–And I were the only boy!'

Then a red light drew his attention to Fories again. Together they turned for the west and home. The show was over. They left the lines with its smoke and death behind; passed over the same rain-sodden fields, with the same working parties slaving at the trenches, and, in quarter of an hour, reached the aerodrome. Warton made a thoroughly bad landing, and broke one of the V-struts of his undercarriage.

Fories looked grave when he heard that Savage and his partner had not yet returned. 'Two hours and a half,' he said. 'They should be home by now. Hope they're all right.' He lit a cigarette and stared frowning into the east.

Warton turned to his observer with an expression of anxious inquiry. Lastor's face was as calm and untroubled as ever. 'No need to worry,' he said reassuringly. 'Savage'll get home.'

At that moment it struck Warton that he had never seen Lastor in the slightest degree worried or lacking in confidence. Even the big fight where Mellor had gone down in flames, had not served to ruffle his composure. Huns to him were simply moving targets on which to practise his skill; Archie a noisy intruder, to be treated with studied indifference. Lastor, after having landed in a machine riddled by bullet-holes, would tidy himself as though he were going to a dinner-party, and settle down to a volume of Swinburne. As these thoughts ran through Warton's mind, the drone of an engine made itself heard, and the mechanics clustered together, pointing out to each other a black speck that had appeared low down over the trees. Warton swung on his heel with a half-irritated laugh. 'What an imperturbable little devil you are!' he said. 'Now who is this? Savage or Barnes?'

'Savage,' replied Lastor, as he followed.

A few minutes later a machine glided between the hangars, landed perfectly in front of the sheds, and taxied up to its position.

'Yes. That's Savage all right!' murmured Warton, beaming with relief. 'Gad, but he has been shot about though!' Savage climbed slowly out and stood fingering one of the many ragged holes that pierced his wings. The fin bracing wires hung loose from their turnbuckles; the lower aileron control wires were frayed and on the point of breaking. All up the fuselage were splashes and punctures that told of withering machine-gun fire. Ryeward was sitting with one leg thrown over the side, growling in his accustomed manner, and mopping his wrist with a blood-stained handkerchief.

'Got jumped on by half the Circus,' explained Savage, in answer to the inquiries that were shouted at him. 'They suddenly nipped out of the clouds. Barnes bit it straight away and crashed. Then they all attended to me. As usual, the gun jammed. Ryeward here got one—' 'in roaring, raging flames,' interposed Ryeward with deep satisfaction. 'The rest followed up,' continued Savage, 'and we had to shake 'em off by contour-chasing home. There were eight–Pfalz scouts–and we only got one!' Just then he noticed the beaded thread of blood that was trickling down the fabric from Ryeward's wrist. 'By Jove, old man!' he exclaimed. 'I didn't know you were hit! Here, some of you people, give me a hand, and we'll get him down.' There was a rush of eager helpers. Ryeward drew himself back. 'What the devil are you people up to!' he shouted. 'Do you think I'm dead or what? Have you never seen anybody cut their finger before? Let go of me and catch this blasted Lewis instead!'

Having handed down his gun, he climbed out of his seat, and tramped away in the direction of the medical hut, refusing to answer any questions. Savage followed him and the group dispersed.

Examination proved that his wound was only a bad graze on the forearm. He persuaded the doctor that a few days' rest would put him right, and thereafter wandered about with his arm in a sling, more surly than ever.

When the orders arrived from the Wing after dinner that night, the major pulled a long face, and called his officers to him. 'You chaps have got to work hard to-morrow,' he announced. 'Trench-strafing at dawn. Break up infantry columns on the roads with Cooper's bombs. Another show at 11 a.m. And a third at 3.30 pip emma. Sounds cheerful! No reving to-night. You'd all better get to bed early.'

There was a blazing fire in Warton's hut when he entered. Sitting gloomily in front of it, was Ryeward. He did not look up, but spoke in a dull voice. 'I knew something would happen this afternoon. It always does. I was a blasted fool not to get out and get in again. If we'd been shot down, it would have been due to that!' Warton stared.

'What on earth are you babbling about?' he ejaculated.

'I knew something would happen!' continued Ryeward, with the same air of depression. I got into the bus from the right-hand side this afternoon!' Warton laughed and chaffed him all the time he was undressing. But before going to sleep that night, he registered a mental vow to get into his machine from the left-hand side on the morrow, and justified his weakness by thinking: 'There may be nothing in superstition; but only a fool takes risks!'

In that gray half light that precedes dawn, the squadron was roused from sleep and compelled to make ready for flying. The morning mists were changing from red to gold as, one by one, muffled figures left the mess, and walked across the aerodrome. Dew silvered each blade of grass, and the smooth-barked trees shone like columns of bronze. So silent was the earth that every sound made by man rang out with peculiar clarity; the roar of a tested engine became furious, the bark of a machine-gun more strident. Mechanics were lying beneath the machines testing bomb-racks on planes and undercarriages, standing on step ladders leant against the cowling tinkering the engines, or sitting in the pilot's seat ready to give 'contact.' As the crowd of pilots and observers repaired to their flights, the increasing clamour became ever more confusing. A sound of talking and laughing mingled with the rattle of Lewis guns, clanging of Vickers' crank handles, the grunts of men heaving on the propellers, and the splashing of feet on the mud-churned tarmac; while at intervals some engine would break into a roar as it started, or cough protesting at the cold morning air. Then the noise died down when the men climbed into their seats. Chocks were pulled from under the wheels, and mechanics strained at the wings to assist the machines over heavy ground. Flight by flight, in groups of four, they turned into wind, and laboured thunderously into the east.

The lines were almost beautiful that morning. Sunshine and mist softened the angular ruins; like the shattered fragments of some Titan's mirror were the innumerable pools of water.

As on the preceding day, a green light fired by Fories broke the formation up into pairs, and drew Warton close down to the leader. Ignoring Archie and scattered machine-gun fire, they flew steadily east along a road marked by the stumps of poplar trees. Isolated bodies of Germans could be seen moving about, but none of sufficient size to warrant sacrificing a bomb. They had crossed the lines at a thousand feet, and were eight miles into enemy country, before Fories spotted a target of sufficient importance. A slow-moving column of gray appeared from a well-marked side track, and turned west up the main road. Guns, horses, and mounted men followed the infantry. He dropped to five hundred feet and roared on full throttle over their heads. Warton, following closely in his wake, found his machine hurled to one side by a shattering explosion that filled the air with smoke and debris. Four explosions followed in rapid succession. 'Thank the Lord!' thought Warton. 'Fories has dropped all his eggs!' Two of the bombs had landed fairly on the road, leaving swelling masses of dun-coloured smoke. In the clear spaces he could see crowds of men that ran from the road and extended into thin lines. Guns were overturned, horses plunged wildly in the confusion, and two wagons were burning fiercely. Many figures lay motionless in the mud.

Fories was flying very low, turning and twisting, using first the front gun, then the back, on the rapidly extending lines of infantry, so Warton flew farther east along the road, to where the tail of the German column had halted and was taking cover. They were not unprepared to meet him, and a simultaneous burst of murderous fire from six machine-guns riddled his machine from wing tip to wing tip. With a sharp clang, some object burst through the petrol tank beneath his seat and ripped open the ankle of his flying-boot, and immediately following it he felt a burning pain along the back of his right hand. He jerked the bomb-releasing lever, and kicked the rudder-bar so as to skid away from the explosion. A beehive-shaped cloud of smoke, mixed with flying lumps of solid, shot up past his right wing. Steadying the machine again, he brought it down to three hundred feet, and released his remaining four bombs in quick succession. For several seconds the earth was blotted out and the air was filled with vapour. The machine rocked and swayed in a sickening fashion, and Warton, cold with horror, crouched forward in his seat. Above the roar of the engine, he heard a high-pitched yell from Lastor, and looked round in time to see him strike some object from off the back of the fuselage. The fabric where the object had been was red and sticky. Suddenly looming through the yellow light appeared a tree trunk. Warton jerked the stick back towards him, and gasped as he rose above the smoky hell into clean air. Machine-gun tracer, fired obliquely from the fields, flashed past underneath and above as he turned west, but he ignored it and flew straight to join Fories, who was still worrying the German infantry. They left the spot, pursued by a few random shots. Looking back over his shoulder,

Warton saw a confusion of black objects scattered round the road, and eight yawning mouths in the earth that breathed slowly and foully. Fories waved cheerfully at him as the two machines swung close in together, but Warton merely nodded in answer, for his teeth were chattering and his knees were loose. Eternity seemed to have passed before they had crossed the lines, and were once again taxying over the hummocky grass of their aerodrome. The major and Fories walked rapidly over to Warton where he stood, dazed and stupid, leaning against the wall of a hangar, and feeling in his pockets for a cigarette. Fories clapped him on the shoulder, saying: 'Jolly good effort, Warts! Damn good! Absolutely spoilt their morning for 'em. Perfectly priceless show! But you mustn't drop bombs from so low again. I thought you were gone. You disappeared completely into the smoke and stuff. Jolly good!'

Warton smiled and moved away to help Lastor take the gun off its Scarfe mounting. He arrived in time to hear a mechanic, as he touched the red patch on the fuselage, say: 'Gad, sir! You haven't been hit have you?'

Lastor shivered slightly, but answered carelessly: 'No. That's where a large chunk of Hun hit us!' For the first time since he landed, Warton noticed that the fingers of his right hand were numb and that the inside of his gauntlet felt warm and wet. He pulled the glove off, and discovered a nasty gash that reached from wrist to knuckles. Walking over to the medical hut, he was stopped by the major, who examined the cut and said, 'Hm, well! There's not much damage done there. Go and get it cleaned up by the doctor. Of course, you won't be flying again to-day.' 'But, sir—' began Warton. 'There's no "but" about it,' interrupted the major. 'That cut on your hand's nothing. But you've done enough to-day, and Lastor's looking as though he'd seen a ghost.' 'But, sir—' 'That's enough, Warton. Go and get your hand seen to.' As he entered the medical hut, Warton slammed the door viciously.

That afternoon, he did not fly, nor for many days after, for in the evening he developed a bad sore throat and a temperature that kept him in bed. There he lay for very nearly a week, talking to Lastor, and worrying Savage with questions concerning each day's work. The fury of the German offensive had abated, and it was generally felt that the crisis had passed. There followed a period of a fortnight, during which rainy weather restricted the squadron's activity to occasional offensive patrols. They moved back north to the aerodrome where they had previously been stationed, and, by the end of the first week in May, were once again established in comfortable quarters. Huns were but rarely met, and seemed generally indisposed to fight. Day after day passed during which the only events had been a few games of ping-pong, and the singing of squadron songs after mess in the evening.

Warton was thoroughly bored, and complained bitterly of the weather. Whenever there was the slightest chance of success, he went up with Lastor, and flew about the lines looking for the 'lone Hun.' He saw a large number of British artillery machines, but never sign of a Hun.

Then one day, in the squadron office, he glanced at the leave roster. His name was next on the list but one among the pilots, and Lastor's was in the same position among the observers. He ran all the way to his hut, and burst in breathless. 'Hi, I say! Lastor! You and I are next but one for leave! Old Savage is due to go in a few days' time. We shall get away in a little over a fortnight!' He had expected his news to electrify his hearers, but the result was a disappointment. Savage put Blackie on to the floor, leant his chin on his hands, and stared at him.

'To think that this creature should be human,' he remarked thoughtfully. 'Have you been deaf or blind or merely normal during the last week? Lastor and I have repeatedly pointed out to you the interesting fact you have just discovered. But were you interested?

Not a bit! You still went pestering round flying in impossible weather, and looking for wretched Huns that never existed. The man's mad!' he concluded, after a pause. Then turned his back to Warton and snored profoundly.

This discovery of the imminence of leave radically altered Warton's views. He prayed for rainy weather when formerly he had cursed it; hoped he would never meet the Hun he had sought so eagerly; ticked off each day on a calendar; went through his kit to see what clothes were there; and wrote to his tailor's, ordering a quite unnecessary new uniform.

'Say, Lastor!' he said one evening. 'Rather a stroke of luck our getting leave together, isn't it? You made any definite plans? I suppose you'll be staying with your people, eh?'

'Can't,' answered Lastor. 'My people are in India, as I've told you before. I shall have to stay with an aunt in Eastbourne. Pretty dismal prospect.'

Warton thought of the invitation given him by Patrick at Boulogne on the first day of his arrival in France. He coughed, and stammered awkwardly. 'Well–er–look here, old bean! Of course, I shall go home first, and–well, the fact is you see–I've only got a pater, and he's a funny old man who likes to be alone.–But a fellow I knew at school told me to drop down at his place for leave and take a friend. Will you come–say for a week?'

'Thanks very much,' said Lastor gruffly. 'You fix it up and I'd like to.'

Savage went on leave, and still the weather remained bad. Three days before Warton and his observer were due to go, the weather changed, and the squadron were required to do two offensive patrols a day. Every time Warton left the ground he felt quite convinced that he would never return alive. The hours spent over the lines were never-ending; his engine always seemed about to fail; and imagination turned every machine in the sky into an enemy. In the mess, too, the manner in which some one would remark carelessly,

'By the way, Warts, you're for leave to-morrow, aren't you?'–struck him as being callous and inconsiderate.

As he was putting on his flying clothes the afternoon before he expected to go, the Recording Officer poked his head in through the window and said, 'Your warrant's come through, Warts. So's Lastor's. You can both cross to-morrow. Fories says you needn't go on this show, if you don't want to.'

'Right! Thanks!' replied Warton, and aimed a mighty blow at a pair of slacks that were hanging over a clothes line, to prevent himself from shouting with joy.

'Hear that, Lasts?' he inquired in a low voice. 'We're both to cross to-morrow!'

'Yes,' replied Lastor calmly. 'But are we going to fly to-night?'

Brilliant spring sunshine poured in through the open window, and the glimpse of sky it revealed was traversed by minute high clouds like mackerel scales. Warton sat down on his bed and sighed. 'Can't say I want to,' he said doubtfully. 'Tell you what would be rather a rag though. It's a topping afternoon. Let's go up and do a show by ourselves. We needn't go over the lines, if we don't want to.'

Lastor acquiesced, so they hurried over to the aerodrome, and got away before the patrol had left the ground. As they climbed, Warton sang continually to himself. He had never felt so happy in his life. Half France, with its green fields and dark blue woods; its villages and sprawling towns; its long straight roads and steel-like canals, seemed to be spread like a map below them. As ever, along the lines were the two antagonistic rows of observation balloons, fat, motionless, and watchful. Away to the north-west, across the belt of sea, stretched the coast of England. Warton pointed it out to Lastor with a grin. They flew very nearly up to the coast, then turned with the wind behind them, and crossed the lines at the Forest of Nieppe. They were at 18,000, when Warton felt himself struck sharply on the shoulder, and looked round to see Lastor pointing at a small machine with extensions on the top plane that was diving on them from the western sun. Two streaks of tracer flashed past between the wings; but no more followed. Lastor's gun cracked once and then stopped. The German scout pulled out of its dive and climbed above them in a very fine turn. 'Some pilot, that!' thought Warton as he watched. No trace of anxiety tinged his mind. He admired the beautiful little machine, as it gleamed in the sun and displayed its polished body of cream and black. In the back seat, Lastor was methodically repairing his gun. Down came the German again. This time Warton turned in to meet him, pulled up the nose of his machine sharply as the enemy passed overhead, and pressed his gun lever. Two shots rang out and then silence. In that moment Warton felt fear. To be fighting a German scout in single combat the day before going on leave, was in itself unpleasant; but to discover simultaneously that his opponent was an expert, and that both guns were jammed, was positively terrifying. He had a passionate desire to turn west, trusting to his own speed and his opponent's inaccurate shooting to get clear away, but he bit his lip and fought it down. Instead, he turned furiously on the German, and flung his machine around in turn after turn, climbing and diving, slipping first to one side, then to the other, as he strove to keep out of the scout's gun-sight. Yet time and again the German all but got that direct shot that would have ended the fight, and each time as he swerved aside, Warton felt his backbone tingling in anticipation of a bullet. He himself, if his guns had been working, could have poured lead into the enemy as he rushed across from the side or climbed up under his nose. Warton was wet from the exertion and praying for the arrival of another British machine, or that the Hun would get frightened and go home. Lastor fired every Very light he could find at the elusive little machine, and then hurled the pistol at it.

Suddenly there flashed a thought through Warton's mind. Acting on impulse, he dived west, half expecting a stream of bullets to riddle him. Not a shot came past. He turned the machine so as to see past the tail, and perceived a small black speck that disappeared rapidly into the east.

When they had reached home, and were gliding down, he leant back and shouted to Lastor. 'Gad! But wasn't that funny? The old Hun had jammed guns as well, and daren't break away from us, any more than we dared break away from him. We were fooling round each other for ten minutes.'

They landed, and having strolled over to the mess, ordered a couple of cocktails. 'Here's to our leave!' said Lastor, raising his glass.

'May it be perfectly good!' returned Warton piously.

They linked arms and returned to the hut. 'Now then, boy,' Warton said as they went. 'We are about to go on a journey in a few hours' time. Shall us pack?'

'Let's!' answered Lastor.

Leave

'So that's England,' said Warton, with his eyes fixed on the distant wall of cliffs. 'Pretty little place, isn't it?' The pair were leaning over the ship's railing, alternately watching the sparkling water and the slowly-approaching land. The sea was unruffled by any breath of air, and overhead there sailed, solemn and portentous, a large 'blimp.' Very few men were crossing on this boat, for, as yet, general leave from France was not being granted; but, nevertheless, each side of the ship was crowded with individuals who gazed eagerly at the ribbon-like shore of home.

To pass the time until they landed, Warton and Lastor reviewed the events of the day, inconsequently and without sequence.

'Pity we missed old Savage at Boulogne,' Lastor remarked. 'Wouldn't he have been sick at seeing us just going on leave when he had just returned?'

'Yes. Not such a bad place, Boulogne. And a jolly good lunch they give you on these boats. Topping day, too! Gad! D'you know, the afternoon show will be just about crossing the lines now!'

'Poor devils! Wonder if they'll meet any Huns. What time do we get to London?'

'About six o'clock. Do you realise that five hours ago we were waiting for the tender outside the mess?'

'Funny to think of, isn't it? But not nearly so funny as to think that we needn't think of thinking of going back for another fortnight. Phew! Give me air, some one!'

'I like your clear way of expressing yourself. Now, look here, about our arrangements. I'll fix up for us to meet at Maidenhead in a week's time. That O.K.?'

'Yes. Only let me know as soon as you can, so's I can give my ferocious aunt the slip.'

At the landing stage they were both struck by the fact that the porters wore a uniform and talked in English. Little boys, in peaked caps, carried baskets displaying magazines whose covers were ornamented with the familiar figure of the 'English Summer Girl.'

'Jove! doesn't this bring home home to one!' Warton remarked idly turning the leaves of half a dozen he had just bought. Both men were seated at a small table in a dining-car that slid, rapidly accelerating, through Folkestone out into the open country. Tea was brought; then came a period of cigarette-smoking, during which neither spoke, but leant back in their seats and stared out of the windows. Golden sunset light glimmered between the hop-poles, throwing long shadows from tree and cottage. It was very nearly dark when the train pulled up at Victoria, where a crowd of anxious civilians, mostly women, awaited its arrival. Warton and Lastor pushed their way through the medley of luggage, embracing couples, and nonchalant porters. It seemed that every one was either laughing, crying, or doing both simultaneously. They parted outside the station, Lastor to visit a friend, Warton to get a taxi to his home. His porter secured one for him in a very short time, and the man touched his cap as the bags were being strapped on.

'Glad to see you home safe again, sir,' he said. 'Where for, sir? Chelsea? Well, seein' as 'ow you're jest 'ome from the front, we'll make it only seven bob.'

Warton grunted and slammed the door. 'Gad!' he murmured, throwing his cap into a corner. 'But this also brings home home to one!'

He was surprised to find London had changed so little during the ages that had elapsed since his departure. The pavements were thronged as before by hurrying crowds. The number of gloating women that hovered round the shop windows was not diminished. He felt, on being thus brought into sudden contact with an activity and set of emotions alien to his own, an indefinable sense of antagonism, as though he had grown old in a foreign country. Yet he was still young enough to hope that the people would notice his kit beside the driver, and realise that he was just back from France.

Arrived at the small house in Chelsea where he and his father had lived for many years, he jumped out, and, refusing to pay his taxi man more than the stipulated seven shillings, sent that worthy grumbling away.

His father was standing in the doorway. 'Hallo, dad! Got home all right, you see.'

'Hallo, my boy! Shall I give you a hand with your luggage? I hope you didn't overpay the cabman. They're very extortionate nowadays.'

Father and son shuffled into the hall, carrying a heavy valise between them. Their housekeeper, a corpulent old woman inappropriately called Mrs Bones, appeared from nowhere, and shook Warton warmly by the hand.

'Well, well! Master Jimmy!' she exclaimed, clucking her tongue. 'Lord! Ain't he grown! Fancy your shooting down that German! There now! Didn't I always say Master Jimmy was flying? And Mrs Stubbs declaring that it was the mechanics that flew, the orficers sitting on the ground giving orders and such like. What a thing to say, to be sure! Now, Master Jimmy, you must sit down and have tea. I've got some of your favourite marrow jam.'

'Thanks very much, Mrs Bones, but I think it's a bit too late for tea. Look, it's nearly half-past six.'

'Fancy now! Who'd have thought it. I've been that worked up this afternoon. Well, you'll enjoy your dinner all the more, I dessay.'

Warton and his father sat down and talked. On his part, Warton described France, the squadron, the major, Savage and Lastor, fights in the air and ground strafing, in short, all the experiences and impressions he had acquired during the past three months; his father described home politics, the vagaries of munition workers, potato queues, and other absorbing topics of the day in his dryly humorous manner. There was but one point of resemblance between father and son, that was their big frames and sturdy build. Mr Warton wore a grizzled gray moustache and was inclined to baldness. His eyes were deep sunk and shrewd; his lips twisted into a perpetual half-sarcastic smile. He was a retired schoolmaster, but in his days of activity had been renowned rather as an athlete than a scholar.

The morning following his arrival, Warton went round to Cox's and investigated his account there. Sixty pounds stood to his credit. He drew out fifteen, and walked into the street feeling a rich man. A large poster plastered up outside one of the theatres struck his eyes. Across the top of the poster, in letters a foot high, was written, 'Thumbs Up!' Underneath was the picture of a girl, whose eyes were bigger than her mouth, peeping through a gaily-coloured hoop at the passing traffic. She wore a green and yellow skirt trimmed with white fur that reached to her knees, and her legs, from knees to ankles, were of extraordinary length.

It was a type of poster of which a thousand variations may be seen all over London as advertisements for anything from a motor-car to a patent medicine. Warton was not attracted. He glanced across the road, and saw another theatre whose posters depicted a staff captain wearing wings on his tunic and spurs on his field boots about to shoot himself with a horse pistol. At the feet of the staff captain lay a woman in evening dress. 'It's a choice between a mellow chorus and a melodrama,' said Warton to himself. Pleased with the feeble epigram, he went into the box office of 'Thumbs Up!' and bought two stalls.

That evening he dined with his father at Maniani's. The entrance to the restaurant seemed to be the scene of numerous chance meetings, and many ladies who had entered with a somewhat vague though speculative manner, he afterwards observed dining with some male friend whom they had been fortunate enough to encounter. There was very little music, although the band played incessantly. His father regarded him quizzically across the table. 'Has this changed at all since you were here last?' he inquired.

'Not a bit,' answered Warton with a chuckle. 'Only it strikes me as being a little funnier. That's all!'

At the theatre he could discover no new features whatever in the entertainment. The same chorus appeared again and again, only in different costumes. They stretched out their arms and nodded their heads in time to the music, while the heroine, dressed as a Chinese idol, and the hero, wearing a powder-stained dinner jacket, sang a duet entitled 'Roses and Cream.' They linked arms and marked time with one foot during a song delivered by a big man wearing a red kilt and a busby, and with shrill voices sang the chorus–'"What ho!" roared the British lion, "I'll strafe the Hun!"' They formed up in a long line holding each other's waists, and ran round the stage led by the funny man who recited a patter song called 'Hunt the Pussy Cat!' In fact, the sentiment, patriotism, and humour were mingled in the same proportions, expressed in much the same words, and by exactly the same gestures, as he had seen in a dozen previous shows, and could have seen in as many then running simultaneously.

Warton was disappointed. In some indefinable way he had expected to see something different, or to derive greater pleasure from the theatre, since his return from France. At the conclusion of the performance, every one waited for the National Anthem to be played, with the exception of a few richly-bejewelled women and cigar-smoking plutocrats who pushed their way past the officers standing at attention. Then, as the last note died away, dozens of subalterns turned to assist adjacent flappers into their wraps, before they performed the same office for the flappers' mothers. Laughing and talking, the audience gathered round the entrance in groups that denied all movement to the few individuals who desired to hurry away. The streets were very dark. Warton was feeling restless and depressed, and, seeing that this was his first day of leave, very annoyed with himself on that account. He wondered what sort of a day Savage had spent, and whether the squadron had shot down any Huns. It seemed curious to him as he caught snatches of conversation from the crowd, that they should be so preoccupied by the horror of war and the danger of air-raids, when they never had to get up at dawn wondering if they would be burnt to death in a flaming machine before sunset. He was still pondering deeply on this question when he got into bed that night.

The following day he heard from Mrs Dowers, Patrick's mother, saying that she and her husband would be very pleased to see both him and Lastor, and that, moreover, they hoped his father would join the party. Warton showed his father the letter, saying: 'I should like you to meet young Lastor, dad. My observer, you know. An awfully stout fellow, and very interesting to talk to.'

Mr Warton agreed to spend the last five days of his son's leave at Maidenhead, and so the matter was arranged.

A week soon passed; so soon, that Warton had hardly realised that he was home, before the day arrived on which Lastor was to join him in London for the journey to Maidenhead. He went to Victoria to meet the Eastbourne train, and took Lastor home with him for lunch. It amused him greatly to observe how his father treated his guest as though he were a man of advanced years and settled opinions. But he was also surprised by the ease with which Lastor talked on every subject, and the knowledge that he displayed.

During the journey to Maidenhead that afternoon, the two discussed their experiences of the last week, and their prospects for the next. 'Had a good time so far, Warton?'

'Oh, yes. Fair to middling. Been to a few shows, and stayed in bed every morning till ten o'clock. Oh, by the way. I got caught in the tube a few nights ago during an air-raid, and got hooted by a lot of aliens for being in R.F.C. uniform. Darned funny! What have you been doing?'

'Oh, just fooling round, you know; studying Yiddish from the crowds in the street. Enormous number of Jews down there. They voss v'rightened by the air-raids, they voss!'

At Maidenhead station they were met by Mrs Dowers. She was a large lady, generous in build and disposition, and was obviously glad to see them. 'Well, Jimmy,' she exclaimed, seizing Warton by both hands. 'It is a pleasure to see you again. It is simply ages since you were here last. So this is Mr Lastor! How d'you do! How very nice for you both to be flying together. I always think one must want someone to talk to up there.' So she prattled on while the luggage was being piled on top of a cab, and Lastor was surreptitiously searching frantically in his pocket for a suitable tip. On the way up to the house from the station she continued to talk incessantly, asking many questions but never waiting for an answer. 'Now, you boys must tell me all about your adventures. You've no idea how excited I get when there's an aeroplane about! How long have you got? Only a fortnight, I expect. It really is a shame how little leave they give. If I had my way—there goes one of those horrible munition people! Oh, my dears, you've no idea how overrun the place is with them. Simply swarming everywhere. Of course, they're all quite impossible! Now do tell me, Jimmy, how were you treated out there? Was your C.O. a nice man? I do hope so, because some of them are so strict. Poor Patrick's had a dreadful time with his. Oh, of course, he told me he had seen you in Boulogne. Now wasn't that a lucky meeting! And that red-headed friend of his, what's-his-name! Patrick used to call him Bunny. Such a nice, quiet young fellow. By the way, we shall be quite a large party here. Jimmy, you remember Betty, of course? And there's a friend of hers, Violet Leslie; a charming girl. And to-morrow there's a captain somebody coming down. I always forget names! Then, of course, your father will be here soon. And–why, here we are at the house!'

They were greeted by Mr Dowers, who was even larger than his wife. He had a pleasant, round face, a jovial manner, and a habit of punctuating his remarks by bursts of hearty laughter.

He grasped Warton's hand warmly as he entered, slapping him on the shoulder the while.

'Hallo, youngster!' he shouted. 'Oh, of course, I forgot; you're a man now! So this is your friend! I'm glad to see you both. So you've both been having a jolly good week up in town, eh? Oh, you can't tell me! I know what you young fellows on leave are like! Particularly you flying men!' This thought appeared to please him greatly, for he was still chuckling when they entered the drawing-room for tea. Two girls rose to greet them, and were introduced by Mrs Dower. Lastor selected a seat between them, and talked pleasantly and without a trace of shyness. Warton sat opposite, balancing a large sandwich on a very small saucer, and at the same time endeavouring to pay attention to Mr Dower's flowing conversation. From time to time he would catch one or other of the girls regarding him critically, and each time he turned hot and red. He felt distinctly annoyed with Lastor for the easy way in which he engaged their attention. Betty he remembered as a flapper whom he had tolerated with profound contempt in the days when he used to visit the Dowers' from Mellbridge. She had her hair up now, and was most disconcertingly pretty. The other was pretty also, and Warton found himself hoping that she and Lastor would get on well together.

In the course of the evening he discovered that Betty had been working in a canteen since the outbreak of war, and was now home for a rest. Her friend had been driving an ambulance for the wounded. He talked to them about flying, and they were politely interested; Lastor talked about the one-step, and they were enthusiastic. By the end of the evening, Warton felt thoroughly depressed, and even began to wish secretly that he had left Lastor to the mercy of his aunt in Eastbourne. When they were going to bed that night he inquired casually: 'Well, old bean, how do you like the people down here?'

'Oh, topping! Awfully good sorts!' replied Lastor.

Warton bent down, and bestowed great care upon the untying of a bootlace. 'And–er–which of the girls do you like best?' he asked.

'Betty, every time!' came the answer promptly. 'I think she's absolutely priceless. Of course, the other girl's awfully nice too. I think you and she would get on very well together, Warts.' Warton suddenly turned out the light and got into bed.

At the end of two days the rivalry that had grown up between the two, and the competition for Betty's favour, bid fair to spoil both their leaves and their friendship. It was clear to Warton that, although Betty liked him, she always preferred Lastor's company; also, that Lastor was beginning to avoid him or to form plans that would keep him away from Betty. He looked so worried and miserable, that when his father arrived he was accused of 'building up for a stomach attack,' a form of bilious indisposition to which he had been particularly subject in his boyhood. A certain degree of confidence existed between him and Violet Leslie, for he felt that she understood him. In fact, unconsciously, he played a part before her, the better to gain her sympathy.

The third day after his arrival was brilliantly fine, and, after lunch, Betty announced that she was going on the river by herself. Lastor was out of the room at the time, and Warton in that moment formed a desperate resolve. He waited until he caught Betty alone in the hall, took a deep breath, and plunged into conversation. 'I say, Betty,' he began. 'If you're going on the river by yourself this afternoon and don't mind, I'm doing nothing this afternoon and would like awfully to come with you.' He paused for breath and waited. Betty was pulling on her gloves and smiling.

'Of course, Jimmy,' she said softly. 'But are you sure you wouldn't sooner go out with Mr Lastor?'

'Oh, no!' Warton answered hurriedly. 'We haven't made any plans. And–er–as a matter of fact, I believe old Lastor is engaged for the afternoon.' Betty was still smiling. 'Very well, then,' she said, looking into his eyes. 'Be down at the boat-house at three o'clock. Do you think a punt would be nice?'

'The very thing!' replied Warton, almost shouting with joy. Running upstairs, two steps at a time, he bumped into Lastor on the landing. 'Hallo, Lasts!' he exclaimed. 'Going out for walk?'

'I don't think so,' Lastor answered casually. 'The fact is, I've got rather a rotten headache, and I'm thinking of taking it easy in the garden.' This seemed too good to be true. Warton murmured a few words of sympathy, and went on to his room. He spent half an hour shaving, and brushing his clothes; then left the house by the back door, and climbed over the wall, to avoid passing through the garden. It was a quarter to three when he reached the boat-house. He cleaned one of the punts, piled all the cushions he could find into it, and lay down luxuriously smoking a cigarette. The prospects of the afternoon were singularly pleasing. He would have a clear two hours alone with Betty, and would show her that he was not such a dull fellow as she imagined. Perhaps even he could persuade her to stay out to tea. His thoughts were interrupted by the sound of some one approaching outside. Apparently Betty was punctual. He scrambled to his feet, and prepared a smile of welcome, as a shadow fell across the door and its owner entered. It was Lastor, clad in spotless flannels, and wearing a brilliantly-coloured blazer. For a few seconds neither spoke. Lastor was the first to break the silence.

'Hallo, Warts, old son,' he began briskly. 'Having a quiet smoke by yourself, eh? Topping cool in here, isn't it?' He paused to light a cigarette. 'I've been looking all over the place for you,' he continued, between the puffs. 'I rather think some one wants to speak to you up at the house.'

Warton decided to be bold. 'I'm afraid they'll have to wait,' he said with an embarrassed laugh. 'The fact is, I've promised to take Betty on the river.' There was a note of pride, even of triumph, in his voice. Lastor dropped his cigarette and stared.

'Well, I'm blowed!' he exclaimed at last. 'That's what I've come down here for!' It was Warton's turn to be surprised.

Explanations followed, and finally Warton looked at his watch, saying, 'Jove! It's twenty past three. Shall we toss up as to which of us takes her? Or do you think she isn't coming?'

'Of course she isn't!' returned Lastor a trifle bitterly. 'This is a little joke of hers. We'd better go out together.'

It was with very little enthusiasm that the two drifted down-stream, and moored the punt on a back water not a quarter of a mile away. Each was occupied with his own thoughts, when Warton glanced at the sky and suddenly exclaimed, 'By Jove, Lasts! What a priceless afternoon it would be for a flip! Wonder what sort of time the squadron's having.'

Then Betty was forgotten for three hours, while the two discussed flying in all its aspects, past flights they had been through together, and future ones they looked forward to. The sun was throwing golden shafts of light along the river when they pulled the punt into the boat-house. Walking back to the house, both turned and said simultaneously.

'It's been a topping afternoon,' then laughed heartily.

That evening the Captain 'Somebody,' to whom Mrs Dowers had referred on the day of their arrival, turned up unexpectedly. He was an insignificant little man with a waxed moustache, and he was full of apologies for being two days late. Both Warton and Lastor, after a short conversation, lost all interest in him, and forthwith ignored his presence so far as was possible. Betty offered no explanation concerning the incident of the boat-house, nor was any demanded of her. But Warton noticed certain glances and smiles exchanged between her and Lastor, and concluded that between them, at any rate, there were no secrets. He himself sank into a state of contented misery, contemplated his return to France with satisfaction, and derived a certain lugubrious pleasure from imagining that his life's happiness was being destroyed before his eyes. He used to brood darkly, or twist his lips into a sardonic smile when he thought that Lastor also would shortly be separated from Betty. Every one in the house noticed his depression, and endeavoured to cheer him up in their several ways. Mrs Dowers, who imagined that it was the end of his leave that oppressed him, used to engage him in long conversations about the pleasure of active service, and the jolly time he would have with his 'chums' in the squadron. Mr Dowers developed a habit of slapping him on the back, and saying–'Buck up, young man; you're not dead yet!' Captain Somebody–Warton never troubled to learn his name–regaled every one with descriptions of his emotions and depressions on previous leaves. His father, who understood very well what the trouble was, said nothing and grinned secretly. Betty showed a determination to be friendly and notice nothing, while Lastor used to watch him with a troubled and puzzled expression as though he were trying to solve some problem. On the night before his last day of leave, Warton lay awake for many hours pondering on the situation. It was clear to him that–as he put it–he 'hadn't got an earthly with Betty,' whereas she and Lastor were obviously attracted to each other. Lastor was his greatest friend, and they would soon be flying over the lines together.

'Poor old Lastor,' thought Warton. 'What rotten luck for him to have to leave Betty just now.' He determined to look after Lastor for Betty's sake, and take care that he did not run into dangerous fights.

He would play the role of disinterested friend, and see that things were made smooth for them. In fact, before he left for overseas, he would say a few words to Betty, perhaps hinting sadly at his own tragedy, and endeavour to fix things up between her and Lastor. So pleased was he with this idea and the prospects of self-sacrifice it afforded, that he could hardly wait all during the next day for the evening, for it was then that he had determined to get Betty alone and talk to her. Lastor, on the other hand, was more silent and worried than he had ever been before. Several times, as they packed their kit together, he seemed on the point of making some confidence, and each time he checked himself. It was not a particularly happy day, for the prospects of the morrow hung like a cloud over every one, and consequently every one endeavoured to appear in the best of good spirits. Yet the sky was clear and blue, and young summer shone along the river banks. Mrs Dowers had made up a large parcel of homemade cake and chocolates, which she presented to the pair with many jokes about the subterfuges she had adopted to obtain extra sugar and currants. Old Mr Warton appeared in his happiest vein, firing off epigrams on every conceivable subject, but at times his jokes were rather forced.

Knowing well what a trying evening it was likely to prove, Mrs Dowers had invited in as many officers and girls as she could muster for the purpose of dancing. The moon rose upon a world warm as August, flooding the stars with its pale green light. By twos and threes the guests arrived after dinner, and by nine o'clock the dance was an assured success. All the furniture had been shifted out of the dining-room, whose polished parquet floor rivalled any ball-room. The room was illuminated by candlelight, and, although the blinds were drawn, the effect was reminiscent of dances in pre-war days. Mrs Dowers at the piano, and two violinists, constituted the orchestra. Betty had promised Warton a fox-trot half-way through the evening, and, as he waited, he amused himself watching the habits and mannerisms of those about him. He noticed a girl who had large feet and sat with them tucked well underneath her chair; while another, the conscious possessor of a very beautiful throat, was persistently watching the moths that fluttered round the ceiling. A middle-aged blonde was sitting in a dark corner, talking coquettishly with an artillery major, and skilfully using her fan to conceal the 'salt cellars' in her neck. Nor were these little vanities confined to the women present. One young subaltern folded his arms and stood under the strongest light he could find, so that the shadows of his deep sunk eyes and firm chin should be well in evidence. Standing nervously near the door was a Scottish captain, who was always screwing a monocle into his eye, and taking it out whenever any one looked at him. Betty danced with most of the men, once with Lastor, and several times with Captain Somebody. When it came to his turn to claim her, Warton felt his heart beating violently, and he was terribly afraid lest his forehead should be shining. As he approached her, he slipped on the polished floor, and ended the journey with an ungraceful skating motion.

'Our dance, I think, Betty!' he mumbled, as soon as he had recovered. Betty pretended to study her programme minutely so as to hide her mirth. 'I say, Betty,' Warton continued, 'I can't dance this beastly dance. Shall we go out on the terrace for a bit? It's a top-hole evening.'

'I should love to, Jimmy,' she answered. 'It's so hot in here, isn't it? And there's a simply gorgeous moon to-night.' When they had reached the terrace and were leaning over the balustrade that faced the garden, Warton was so excited by the moonlight, the proximity of Betty, and the sound of the music that came from the house, that he was completely deprived of the power of speech. He mopped his forehead and thought to himself, "Strewth! This is just like some beastly scene out of a rotten book!' Several times he opened his mouth to speak, but only succeeded in clearing his throat. Betty seemed quite unconscious of his embarrassment. She gazed at the shining river and the soft black shadows in the garden, while Warton looked at her and thought how 'ripping' the moonlight looked on her neck and arms. Then she turned towards him and sighed. 'Oh, Jimmy!' she said. 'Isn't it a perfect shame you've got to go to-morrow?' Warton sighed, too, and looked at the moon. The resolves he had formed the night before were melting like snow in the sun.

'I say, Betty,' he began suddenly. 'You know we've known each other for an awfully long time. Have you noticed anything funny about me since I came down here?' Betty looked startled.

'Good heavens, no, Jimmy!' she exclaimed. 'Why, whatever do you mean?'

'Well, I don't mean funny exactly, only–oh, hang it all, Betty–you must have seen I wasn't giving full revs–all of a doo-da kind of!'

'Yes, I know, Jimmy,' she answered, moving closer to him, and touching his hand gently. 'You've been so sad and strange. Do you mind going back to France so awfully? Is there anything I can do?' Warton gulped with emotion, clasped her hand firmly in his, and picked leaves from the ivy that grew round the balustrade.

'Yes, there is,' he announced desperately. 'Betty, you must know I'm fearfully fond of you and all that!' The hand he held wriggled slightly, and Betty said:

'Well, Jimmy?' in a low, even hopeful voice. Warton gabbled rapidly on.

'And because we're such old friends, Betty, I want to say that old Lasts is a topping fellow, and I'm glad you and he get on so well together. And as we're going to-morrow, if there's anything I can do to help you and him–He's a splendid fellow and no end of a fine shot with a Lewis gun–and–' His voice trailed off into silence. Betty was laughing as she pressed his hand.

'Oh, Jimmy! You really are a perfect dear! Now, run along, because my next dance is with Mr Lastor, and I believe he's coming out to look for us.' Warton left her, and, as he passed Lastor coming down the steps, felt happy in the accomplishment of a good action. Having joined Betty, Lastor promptly spoke in a solemn voice.

'Miss Dowers–by the way, may I call you Betty?–there is something I particularly want to say to you.' He paused, and kicked the ground while Betty watched him out of the corner of her eye. 'You may think it awful cheek of me to speak to you about a matter like this after I've only known you for such a short time, but, perhaps, as I'm going away to-morrow, you won't mind, will you?'

Betty shook her head and murmured very softly, 'No. I don't think I shall mind.'

Lastor possessed himself of her hand, and she made no effort to withdraw it. 'Well, now, what I want to say is this. Old Warts–Jimmy, I mean–is an absolutely A1 fellow, and he's most awfully fond of you. He's absolutely miserable now. But if you kind of helped him a bit, it would buck him up no end. Do you think you can?' Betty pulled her hand sharply away, and commenced to move towards the house.

'I really can't think what's the matter with all you men to-night. You're all absolutely mad!'

Lastor followed her, hurt and surprised, and spent the remainder of the evening sitting by himself behind the piano. When the dancers had all gone, Mrs Dowers gathered her guests round the sideboard and poured them out a glass of wine each.

'I have a great surprise for you all,' she announced. 'I want you to drink to the health of an engagement–my daughter Betty and Captain Browne.' Warton and Lastor stared for a few seconds at the little man whom they had previously called Captain Somebody; then raised their glasses and drank to his health. They talked long into the night, and for the first time they called each other by their Christian names.

'I say, Jimmy, old son,' said Lastor, as he turned out the light, 'we've nearly made silly asses of ourselves on this leave. On the whole, I'm darned glad we're going back to France to-morrow!'

'So 'm I,' replied Warton in a very sleepy voice. 'Good-night and *beaucoup* Huns!'

War

It happened that the departure of their boat from Folkestone on the following day was postponed from the morning to the afternoon. Warton and Lastor, therefore, spent many hours wandering round the town, or sitting in deck-chairs facing the sea, while aeroplanes by squadrons and flights hummed slowly by overhead and disappeared into the iron-gray mists of the channel. The town was very crowded, particularly with those about to return to France, and there was also a large number of wounded men, who lay in the sunshine chewing blades of grass, or were wheeled about in bath-chairs. As the two left the marine parade and walked down to the boat they were pursued by the music of a band playing 'Here We Are Again!' The routine of embarkation and the seemingly endless period of waiting before the boat finally cast off her moorings, and steamed out into the harbour, damped Warton's spirits more than anything else had done since leaving Maidenhead. He sat staring at the wake, and sucking the stem of an empty pipe. 'Cheer up, man!' said Lastor, suddenly noticing his air of depression. 'We shall be getting grub in Boulogne with old Savage soon! By the way, did you see Betty again after last night?'

'Nope!' came from Warton. Then a long pause. 'Gad, wasn't it beastly leaving by that milk train this morning? Why the devil do they want to drag us up to Victoria at 7.30 in the morning, and then keep us waiting round Folkestone all day? Can you imagine what she wanted to get engaged to that awful little tick of a captain for?'

'No, I can't! Confound the girl, let's talk of something else. If this weather lasts we ought to get some scrapping. Scrapping means Huns, and Huns mean all sorts of things. You've got four so far, haven't you?'

'Yes, poor devils! D'you know, I can't help feeling sorry for those Huns. After all, they were human, I suppose!'

Lastor snorted contemptuously. 'You've still got one or two things to learn about war, old son!' he replied.

So they talked until the boat thumped alongside the quay at Boulogne. The town, vociferous and smelly as ever, with its cobbles and railway trucks running through the streets, made home seem very far away. And Savage, standing in his accustomed attitude, feet wide apart, hands thrust into the pockets of an oily old waterproof, hat over one eye, and a pipe gripped between his bared teeth, was almost the first man they saw on crossing the gangway. The familiar figure and the familiar background gave the lie to the passage of time. It seemed impossible that they had been on leave, or that the many events of the past fortnight had taken place. Surely it was but a few hours ago that they had left the squadron, and that this was the end of a day's expedition into Boulogne. Something of Warton's thoughts must have been reflected in his face, for Savage as he shook hands remarked: 'Enter one perfectly good damned soul into purgatory! All hope abandon ye who enter here! Hallo, Lasts, you're looking pretty chirpy also! By way of celebrating this auspicious occasion, I have engaged a table at Mony's. We will now have the odd champagne cocktail and so to dinner. The tender's just round the corner. Chuck your bags into it and come along.' As they walked towards the restaurant, Savage made several attempts to get either one or the other of his companions to talk, but, receiving only monosyllables in answer, abandoned the attempt and kept the conversation entirely to himself.

'We've been having no end of a time since you went,' he announced. 'Huns simply all over the sky, and very ferocious. We've had to teach them better manners on several occasions. Old Fories has now got a round dozen, and his M.C. to boot. What's more, we haven't lost a single machine. You two will enjoy your little selves!'

When he took off his coat and sat down at the dinner table, Warton and Lastor simultaneously noticed a very new white-and-purple ribbon beneath his wings. Each seized a hand and pump-handled it vigorously. 'Steady on, steady on!' protested Savage, 'you'll damage my sword arm for life if you go on like that, Warts! Now, what are we going to drink? How about some Veuve Clicquot?'

Although Savage's decoration had pleased them both immensely, the end of their leave still acted as a drag upon their spirits, and silences were frequent. 'It is my firm conviction,' Savage announced, nibbling an olive–that you have both fallen in love. Oh, my poor young friends. "*Croyez moi j'ai passé par là!*" The same thing happened to me on leave. Only she wore pins in her waistband so I left her for ever. Are you both going to have *sole meunière?*'

Warton blushed guiltily, and turned the conversation into flying topics. They left Boulogne shortly after ten, and, on arriving at the aerodrome, went straight to bed without having entered the mess, whence issued the usual sound of singing and scuffling.

The next morning they reported to the major and to Fories, both of whom inquired whether they had had a good leave; unpacked their kit; took a machine up and flew round the aerodrome a few times; then settled down to the old routine of squadron life. On the evening patrol, they crossed the lines by the Forest of Nieppe, and flew towards Lille. The ground below shone gold and green in the sun, and the sea to the north shone blue and green. It was very like the afternoon before they had gone on leave. Warton found himself wondering what the Hun who had attacked them on that occasion was doing, and whether he were still alive. Then he wondered how his observer was feeling, and looked round. Lastor was slowly swinging the gun with his left hand, and screening his eyes with his right to gaze into the sun. Standing up in his seat for a moment to look over the centre section, Warton saw some black specks far away in the east. Instinct told him that they were Huns, also that they were approaching. He felt curiously cold and fretful as he fired an unnecessarily long burst from his gun to warm it up; then absurdly angry with the Huns for existing at all. As Fories skilfully manoeuvred so as to get the sun behind him, Warton found himself swearing under his breath and banging his fist restlessly against his knee. It was clear that the enemy had not seen them, for they came unhesitatingly on in a straggling formation that promised but little chance of defence. So blind and careless did they appear, that Warton scented a trap, and searched every quarter of the sky for a high-flying German escort. To the east there was not another machine to be seen, but some distance behind them and below them was a solitary British artillery machine. That explained the Germans' preoccupation; they were too absorbed stalking their defenceless prey to notice Fories' close-packed formation that had at its back the dazzling mist round the sun. Then the enemy formation split up, two machines remaining behind and climbing steeply, the other six spreading out fanwise to surround the artillery machine and engage the pilot's attention, while the two who had gained height should dive upon him. Warton chuckled when he saw this manoeuvre. 'Truly,' he thought, 'the Lord is delivering them into our hands!' Fories with the unerring judgement born of long experience, led his companions down to within five hundred feet of the two topmost Huns. Then he dived. One of them burst into flames with a violence akin to that of an explosion. In a flash the other turned and dived east across the nose of Warton's machine. Warton followed, with his eyes glued to the Aldis sight, his fingers slowly tightening on the gun lever. A little delicate play on the rudder-bar to steady his machine, and the German scout appeared as a stationary silhouette in the centre of the ring. Warton bit his lip as his gun burst into chattering fury, and the stinging smell of oil and cordite filled his nostrils. His fire took immediate effect, for the stricken machine reared up on its tail like a frightened horse, then slowly rolled over sideways on to its back. A black object detached itself from the fuselage and dropped away beneath it. From the shape Warton knew that it was a man. Almost unconsciously he glanced at the altimeter and said to himself: '17,000! He'll be dead before he reaches the bottom.' Meanwhile Fories and the remainder had turned and attacked the six scouts who were stalking the artillery machine. It was a brief contest, for two went down to the first dive, and the remaining four scattered and fled east, hotly pursued by Savage. Warton, coming up to his assistance, was only in time to see one of the Germans dip his nose down and down till it pointed at the ground; then fall vertically and vanish. Of the three that were left, he selected one, swung into his favourite position on its tail, and fired about fifty rounds. Desperate to escape, the German swooped upwards in the first part of a loop, but, before reaching the zenith, the fuselage of his machine bent at its thinnest part, the tail twisted itself and broke off, and the whole machine fell to pieces, fluttering and buckling like leaves in a gale.

That ended the fight. After they had landed, Savage walked over to Warton, shouting: 'Gad! But wasn't that a topping scrap? Six down out of eight! Yours were jolly good Huns too! One bundled out, and the other shot to pieces in the air. Guess they won't trouble us again!'

Warton was silent for a few seconds before replying: 'Confound it all, but it was beastly! You know I hate these melodramatic affairs. When I shoot a Hun down I should like him to only get a Blighty one, and go into hospital for a bit. I don't want the poor wretch to fall out.'

The following day was rainy in the morning, so Warton and Lastor visited the mess of some machine-gunners who were billeted in the neighbourhood, and borrowed a couple of horses. These they obtained in return for a promise that the creditors should go up for a joy-ride. They spent an hour running races over the flat fields, but the sport was brought to an end by Lastor's horse, which suddenly stopped dead and threw him heavily. Lastor picked himself up laughing, and proceeded to brush the mud from his tunic. As he did so, he gave a sharp exclamation, and fingered his right wrist tenderly. 'Now isn't that sickening?' he said. 'I've sprained my beastly wrist again. It's as weak as water. You might catch that brute of a horse, will you, Warts, and I'll get it seen to before it swells up.'

By the afternoon, however, in spite of the attentions of the medical orderly, his wrist was so painful and stiff that he had to carry his arm in a sling.

It was impossible for him to swing a gun-mounting with one arm, and Fories declared that he could ill spare Warton for that show, so it was arranged that Warton should take up Coote, a new sergeant-observer who had recently arrived. Warton sought the sergeant after lunch, to give him instructions, and find out what sort of an observer he might be. He discovered the man sitting in one of the hangars, working on a very crude sketch of the aerodrome. The new observer was a pleasant little man, with a small black moustache. He spoke quickly, and seemed very pleased that he was going to fly with Warton. The latter admired his artistic effort, whereupon Coote produced a large packet from one of his pockets. 'Perhaps you'd like to look through these, sir,' he remarked rather self-consciously, 'they're some drawings by my little son. Cute little nipper he is, sir. Only a six year old.' Warton examined the scrawling reproductions of cows, and railway trains, with as much appearance of enthusiasm as he could assume, made a few banal remarks, and handed them back. 'Thought you'd think 'em good,' said Coote, chuckling with satisfaction. 'He's a rare un is my little nipper!'

Because he was not in the least anxious to meet any Huns that afternoon, Warton felt that it was inevitable that they should do so. In this surmise he was correct, for hardly had the patrol crossed the lines before they encountered a veritable swarm of Fokker triplanes and Pfalz scouts that seemed to appear from every part of the sky. In the ensuing 'dog fight,' Warton was kept busy trying to remedy a chronic double feed in his Vickers gun. The little sergeant, with a piece of half-chewed string hanging from a corner of his mouth, worked feverishly at the back, rattling the magazine on its post, and firing drum after drum at any machine that came near. But his shooting, though enthusiastic, was inaccurate. Warton saw very little of the fight. Unconsciously he used stick and rudder for dive and turn the while he wrestled with the crank handle of his Vickers gun. Whenever he took a hurried survey of the sky he received a confused impression of small, black-crossed machines darting here and there with Fories or Savage in pursuit. He saw one German scout spin slowly down in flames, and several others dive east to take refuge in the clouds. The number of machines was considerably diminished by the time he had remedied the stoppage, and was testing his gun with a short burst. Coote, at the same time, was leaning over the side pouring tracer into a Hun several thousand feet below. Above the din caused by the two Huns, Warton heard a sharp crackling noise and something burst through the fuselage behind him, ripping splinters from the wicker-work of his seat. Coote abruptly stopped firing and fell back against Warton's head, clutching at the empty air with his upraised hands. Then he crumpled up like a doll and lurched forward on to the floor of his cockpit. At the instant at which the bullet struck his seat, Warton had kicked hard at the rudder-bar and skidded away to one side. But over his shoulder he saw a Fokker triplane, painted with black and yellow stripes, that swung round on his tail, almost without ceasing to fire. Warton turned and twisted, trying any expedient he knew to shake off the triplane, but it was all of no avail. The German followed every movement, playing with his two guns upon Warton's machine as with a hose. From below, where they had dived to chase home the stragglers, Fories and Savage watched the duel with anxious eyes, unable to offer any assistance. It was Warton's aim to induce his opponent to overshoot, so as to enable him to use the front gun, but neither loops nor rolls served to lure the German on or to confuse him. At the end of every manoeuvre he was still in the same position, not twenty yards from Warton's tail plane, firing short bursts that frayed the wings, and ricocheted from the engine cowling. Warton had almost forgotten Coote lying motionless in the back seat, so he was the more amazed to see the figure first stir uneasily, then stagger gropingly to its feet. His jaw hung down and saliva dripped from his open mouth; as he stood up, a dark red jelly-like mass slid from the lap of his flying coat on to the floor. Swaying like a drunken man, he pushed up the goggles from his eyes with one hand, and felt round the mounting with the other until his fingers closed uncertainly on the spade-grip of the Lewis gun. Slowly, as though shifting an immense weight, he swung the gun round towards the triplane. Then he laid his cheek against it and aligned his sights. Instinctively, Warton steadied his machine for the shot and waited. The Lewis gun clamoured with its irritated laugh for a few seconds while the blazing tracer leapt across at the German. Warton watched for its effect, panting with excitement; then muttered,–'Ah, God! Good man!'–as the triplane swerved aside and hung poised in the air, before it spun slowly and flutteringly down. When he looked again into the observer's cockpit he saw Coote lying on his stomach across the seat, his knees gathered in close underneath him, his arms held limply up by the bracing wires. Warton throttled back his engine and shouted, but received no reply.

When he reached the aerodrome he helped to lift the wounded man out and carry him into the squadron office, where he was laid on a roll of blankets. The little man was still conscious, and whispering feebly for morphia. The doctor cut away his clothes and revealed a round jagged wound in the left side just below the ribs. 'Explosive bullet!' he ejaculated, and stood up. 'He won't live five minutes.' Warton, in obedience to a request from the dying man's eyes, knelt down to catch whatever words he could say.

'Goo' scrap, sir!' The words came in a strange cracked voice. 'I–got 'im–got 'im–'. The last word trailed off into silence, as he slowly drew one hand out of his tunic pocket, and handed Warton the packet of drawings which he had displayed that afternoon. A ghostly smile flickered round his lips, and his head fell back as the last breath sighed in his throat.

Very white in the face, Warton rose to his feet and turned to the doctor. 'You say it was an explosive bullet?' he asked. The doctor nodded.

'Yes. The dirty swine!' he replied. In that moment there came to Warton a realisation of the meaning of war, and he thereby became many years older. Without removing his helmet he sat down in his hut, and wrote to Coote's wife describing the fight, and enclosing the child's drawings.

For a week after that incident he did not fly, for the major insisted that he should wait until Lastor's wrist permitted him to use a gun again. All the efforts of Lastor and Savage to dispel his depression, and even Ryeward's clumsy sympathy, failed to have any effect. He sat on his bed smoking incessantly, and racking his memory for incidents in the fight that might point to carelessness or lack of skill on his part. He came to the conclusion that in no wise was he to blame for Coote's death, and his fury against the German for using explosive bullets was thereby not diminished. Whereas formerly he had regarded fighting in the air rather in the light of a sport than a serious business, and had wished his opponents no worse ill than a slight wound, he now prayed for the death of every Hun he should encounter. One evening, Savage who had been watching him thoughtfully, broke the silence by saying: 'Yes, Warts, war is a dirty game isn't it?'

'*This* war is!' returned Warton emphatically. 'Why can't men fight fair? Hang it all, we're supposed to be civilised!'

'Exactly,' Savage continued, 'and civilisation simply means a refinement in your methods of hurting your neighbour both in war and peace. Chivalry had as its origin the fact that most men, on being taken prisoner, would sooner lose their money than their life.'

Having no reply to this, Warton relapsed into gloomy silence.

The next occasion on which Warton and Lastor were required to go over the lines, was for the purpose of strafing balloons, a job which pleased Warton but little, for he had set his heart upon shooting more machines down in flames. However, he derived some comfort by obtaining permission to carry four Cooper's bombs, with which he hoped to do some damage. They were fortunate, inasmuch as the day of the balloon-strafe dawned upon a sky wherein floated large cumulus clouds, such as would cover their approach from Archie. Orders had been received that all enemy balloons between two pin-points lying about eight miles apart, should be driven down and forced to remain on the ground for the period of an hour.

Fories left the aerodrome with his flight about two hours after dawn, and noted the position of each balloon along the line, before he climbed through the clouds. With a strong north wind behind him, he intended to rush the balloons from north to south, forcing each one down in the shortest possible time, and trusting to his tremendous ground speed to invalidate the accuracy of fire from the ground. There were five balloons on the strip of ground allotted to them, each one wagging its head solemnly into the wind at a height of four thousand feet. It seemed almost as though an attack had been expected, for over the line itself, while still above the clouds, the four machines were subjected to very searching Archie fire. Fories flew straight on, utterly ignoring the black puffs that stained the white floor of mist.

On previous occasions, Archie had never caused Warton any anxiety, but now he found himself jumping at every burst, and even ducking his head whenever a crack louder than the others accompanied the appearance of a ball of smoke close to his machine. He pulled himself together with an effort, and remembered that he had not been sleeping well recently. Also he resolved that, before going over the lines next time, he would drink a strong whisky and soda. By the time the patrol had reached the balloon line, the sky behind them was black and pimpled by the lingering smoke, and every second brought an explosion closer to one or other of the machines. Warton was suffering from an agony of fear; his knees trembled, and he whimpered like a frightened child at every sound. The sight of the first balloon, fat and tantalising, restored a certain measure of his old enthusiasm. He was glad when Fories shut off his engine, and fell away in a vertical side slip to get within diving distance of the gas-bag. He followed suit, then took careful aim and poured round after round at the paunch-like envelope. His fire had not the slightest effect, but the balloon began slowly to descend.

Looking down, he saw a crowd of men running about in a field directing what looked like a large trolley which moved slowly along its rails, hauling down the balloon as it went. The ground in the vicinity of the trolley sparkled with gun-flashes. Excited beyond the common, Warton failed to notice that his companions were no longer about him, but were engaging a balloon over a mile away. He followed the sinking balloon down, repeatedly diving to within a few yards, then turning so as to bring Lastor's gun to bear upon it. The two occupants jumped out and floated down with their parachutes, looking like two jellyfishes in clear water, but Warton never abated the fury of his attack. He was determined to set the balloon on fire, and bitter tears of vexation lay cold upon his cheeks, as burst after burst was fired without producing the slightest apparent result. The lower he went the thicker came the storm of bursting shells, that filled the air with an intermittent crackling like the rending of a gigantic canvas. Wicked little red bullets chased each other past his wings, and strings of green stars rose from the ground like the bubbles in a glass of soda water.

At a thousand feet, Warton could see the ant-like activity of the men below him, and the progress of the trolley along its rails. It was then that he remembered the bombs that hung waiting upon his racks. Leaving the balloon, he dived for the ground and raced across the field at a few hundred feet, jerking the release lever as he went. Two of the bombs dropped close to the group of Germans, obscuring them with heavy yellow smoke; the other two fell harmlessly upon a neighbouring wood. More furious than ever was the defensive fire, and the explosions from the gun muzzles mingled with those of the shells with a noise as of the banging of innumerable doors. Many of the bracing wires curled loose from their turnbuckles between the planes; splinters flew from the struts, and a gaping rent appeared in one bottom plane. Warton was sobbing quietly to himself and twitching with almost every muscle, as he sprayed the boundaries of the field with fire from his front gun. Lastor, standing serenely up behind him, was still firing incendiary ammunition at the gas-bag. Unable to bear the strain any longer, and having used every cartridge in the belt, Warton turned west at a thousand feet, and zigzagged away. Lastor banged him on the right shoulder, and he was surprised at the sudden acute pain he experienced as he turned round. But the sight that met his eyes made him forget the pain, for instead of the hideous bean-shaped balloon, a cone of scarlet flame, trailing volumes of dense black smoke, was falling to the earth. Warton watched it until it struck the ground and lay smouldering fitfully at the foot of some trees; then he sighed gently and smiled as his eyes met Lastor's. With the exception of a few random shots, they were not worried on their way back to the lines.

Having reached British territory, Warton relaxed the tense watch he had hitherto maintained, and became promptly aware of a numbness that reached from his shoulder blade upwards. He tried to raise his arm, but was stopped by a stabbing pain that made him catch his breath. The inside of his sleeve, also, was warm and wet, and his vest was clinging to his back, and burning as though it were red hot. He glanced at his watch; nine o'clock. It occurred to him that his father, at that moment, was just settling down to his morning paper and breakfast. For no reason, the thought appeared particularly funny. He threw back his head with a laugh, but the laugh was turned into a very different ejaculation as the movement stretched the wound in his shoulder. For a few seconds, every visible object seemed to swing rapidly round his head, and the sky was scarlet instead of blue. The thought that he was going to faint sobered him considerably, and he stared fixedly ahead at the distant aerodrome, unconsciously singing to himself. When he had landed and stopped the engine, he clambered hastily out, missed his footing on the plane, and lurched heavily against the bracing wires, where he stood swaying and chuckling with merriment. Then he noticed that Lastor was being helped down from his seat by two mechanics. 'Got a bullet in the heel,' explained Lastor cheerfully, hopping towards him on one foot.

The battered and bullet-riddled machine, Lastor's comic move-ments, the anxious faces of the mechanics, all combined in Warton's eyes to form a picture of inexpressible humour. 'What! You hit too!' he shouted at Lastor between his bursts of laughter. '*So* glad!' Then darkness broke like a surf over his head, and he pitched forward into the arms of his flight sergeant. It was but a brief fainting spell. He came to, to find himself lying on the blankets in the squadron office, while the major supported his head, and endeavoured to pour some brandy down his throat. Lastor was sitting on a chair in the corner, having his left foot bandaged by the medical orderly.

'How are you feeling, old man?' said the major. 'A bit better, eh? That's fine! Now we'll send you and Lastor down to the Clearing Station, and I expect you'll go home.'

'But I don't want to go home!' Warton burst out fretfully. 'I want to come back. Can't you arrange for me to come back?'

'Oh, yes, I expect so,' the major answered soothingly. 'Now, don't you worry. It was a jolly good show of yours. Here's your batman. Tell him what things you want to take with you, and dictate your report to Astley here.' So Warton lay back and haltingly gave an account of the morning's events. With a little assistance, he walked to the tender, where he sat grinning rather foolishly at Lastor. Every member of the squadron in turn looked in to say a few words, but it was not until the tender had started to move down the road that Warton remembered that he had not seen Savage.

'Hi, stop! Stop!' he yelled, banging the driver on the head with his left arm. The major came running up.

'What the deuce is up now?' he inquired breathlessly. Warton explained, and for ten minutes the pair sat silently in the tender waiting for Fories and Savage to return. Warton's mind was just beginning to form vague apprehensions, when the two machines appeared and landed, and a few minutes later, Savage, with his leather coat flying in the wind, and his big boots clattering as he ran, galloped across the aerodrome and scrambled into the tender.

'Right away!' he shouted at the driver, then turned to Warton and said, 'Hallo, boy! They've only just told me about you. You are a silly ass, you know. I thought you were dead. Whatever made you go down to the ground like that?'

'I dunno,' Warton replied, 'I kind of got annoyed.'

'Well, any way, you got the old sausage,' continued Savage. 'And now how are you feeling? It's only a bit of a cut in the shoulder, isn't it? You, Lasts, too, with a punctured heel! 'Strewth, I could shake the pair of you! Anyway, I'm coming with you to the C.C.S. to make sure you don't start any nonsense on the way. Why, what the devil's that thing coming down the road?' Warton looked back and saw a small figure hotly pursuing them in a cloud of dust. They stopped the tender and waited. 'Well, I'm darned if it isn't old Ryeward!' exclaimed Savage, as the figure approached, and Ryeward, very hot and with his helmet held on top of his head by the elastic of his goggles, leapt at the step of the tender, and fell at full length upon the floor.

'Thought I'd come and see how you were,' he announced, as soon as he was able to speak; and thereafter sat solemnly staring at Warton, alternately growling and puffing his cheeks in and out. The Casualty Clearing Station was only a few miles from the aerodrome, so Savage and Ryeward left the wounded pair at the gate, with promises to return on the following day. Warton and Lastor were taken into a large, cool tent and examined by a brisk little surgeon who was continually dropping his gold-rimmed pince-nez. Lastor's case was soon disposed of.

'Nothing much wrong with you, young man,' he announced. 'A week's complete rest, and a little leave will put you right.' But at the sight of Warton's wound he shook his head. 'Hum!' he said. 'Well, as you *want* to stay in France, I'll try not to send you down to the base. But we'll have to open up that wound of yours first, and see just what damage has been done. Now follow the orderly, both of you, and get to bed.'

The ward in which they found themselves consisted of a long, low tent, with some fifteen or twenty beds aligned along each side. A smiling and gray-haired sister met them, and gave them a couple of beds next to each other. Warton was much embarrassed by her attempts at assisting him to undress, and was greatly relieved when he could slide down between the sheets, and ease the pain of his aching shoulder. But few words were exchanged between him and Lastor, for both were mentally living the morning over again in all its details. But even among the other patients there was very little conversation. Occasionally a man groaned, or the sister, moving silently up and down the ward, whispered a few words as she straightened a pillow or helped a man to change his position. The silence and rest after the devilish clamour of the morning's fight, produced in Warton's mind almost complete oblivion to his surroundings. He was once more listening to the Archie bursts, and watching the flaming balloon, when an orderly tapped him on the chest, and indicated a stretcher lying on the floor between its two bearers at the foot of his bed. 'You're for the operating theatre, sir,' said the orderly in a low voice. 'Can you get up by yourself?'

'Yes, thanks,' said Warton cheerfully, while his heart hammered furiously at his throat. 'I'm quite all right.' He grinned at Lastor as he lay down on the stretcher and was covered with blankets while the sister came up and patted his hand, saying it wouldn't last long. Then he felt himself lifted and carried through the door of the tent, out into the sunshine. The wind blew pleasantly against his temples, and he enjoyed the gentle rocking of the stretcher. He closed his eyes, but opened them again as the sunlight was blotted out, and he heard voices about him. He was in a tent similar to the first but that it was furnished with an operating table surrounded by basins on stands, and a shelf of glittering instruments. The table was walled in by screens, and beyond the screens there seemed to be many more partitions. Warton caught a glimpse of a figure lying swathed under coverings that was being lifted from the table on to a stretcher. On being carried past, he noticed that the man on the stretcher was wheezing as he breathed, and that his skin was of a curious green colour. Then he found himself on the table, staring past a face that bent over him at a little patch of blue sky that was framed in by a ventilator in the roof. Around him he felt the presence of several people and the sound of voices, one of them a woman's, but dominating them all was the personality of the grave-faced man who bent over him. So far, the proceedings had held but little interest for him; he was too absorbed studying the bit of sky overhead. A voice whispering in his ear, roused him from his reverie, and, at the same time, some sort of a bag was pressed over his mouth and nose. The inside of the bag smelt sweet and a trifle sickly. His hand was touched, then held gently; opening his eyes he could just see the apron and forearm of a nurse. The voice in his ear was still saying, 'That's right. Breathe steadily and deep. Good lad. That's right.' There came a metallic clink from behind him, mingled with a surge and beat that dimly he realised must be his pulse. Faster and faster he breathed and the throb of his heart grew more insistent. Overhead the small patch of sky seemed to be shining through a very fine grille of red bars, which grew close and blacker until they obliterated it altogether. The table had fallen away from beneath him, and he was floating in space; no, not floating; rushing backwards and upwards past myriads of stars. From the other side of the stars came a very deep voice saying, 'He's a tough beggar. Give him a shade more.' The hand that held his was tingling now, and had turned cold. Everything about him was moving in the darkness. He sensed their presence but could see nothing.

If he went on travelling backwards at this rate, he would arrive in London head first. That would be funny. That would amuse Betty also. Betty was so fond of the moon, and there was a moon only a few feet away. He could easily catch hold of it if only he could move, but there was something pressing on the bridge of his nose that prevented him from moving. It was fearfully dark, and the soles of his feet were cold. That was because he had stopped travelling backwards, and was falling, falling feet first into eternity. He was frightened, and the soles of his feet were cold. There was that moon still there; just out of reach. It was a curious sort of moon, with a hollow in the middle of it. Some kind of light was shining behind it; the sun, he imagined, through an open door. There was a woman moving about close to him. She looked like the sister. The whole place resembled the ward he had just left, only it was difficult to see, because it would keep spinning round and humming quietly to itself. 'How are you feeling, old bean?' That was Lastor's voice. 'Fine!' answered Warton, as he raised himself on one elbow, and was sick into the basin that had once been the moon.

He slept for the remainder of that day, and consequently lay awake all night, listening to the German night raiders that snored their way across the sky, promiscuously dropping bombs. The pain in his shoulder was acute in degree, though vague in locality, for no matter what position he adopted, the aching part was always directly beneath his weight. The night nurse going her rounds came across Warton stirring uneasily and sighing. She smoothed his pillow and bedclothes, then sat down beside him and talked about England, home, and summer holidays. Warton listened politely, before he announced that nothing would induce him to go home. She was surprised, but could get no explanation.

At last dawn came, throwing olive green shadows in the darkness of the ward, turning pillows and sheets into masses of pale blue light. As the first rays of sunlight glanced along the roof of the tent, Warton heard the engines of his squadron droning eastward to the lines. The surgeon who examined his wound that morning was well satisfied. 'Perfectly clean and healthy,' he said, 'we won't have to send you home after all.' This news pleased Warton so much that he challenged Lastor to a one-armed pillow fight. His challenge, however, was overheard by the sister, and the event never took place. Most of the men in the ward were bad cases, and they lay like logs all day, only occasionally whispering for the sister to help them move a limb. But there was one Scotchman with a bullet hole in his lungs, who sat up in bed supported by a number of pillows, and delivered himself of anecdote after anecdote in a strange, high-pitched voice. The skin of his face was white and stretched close against the skull; his eyes were of unusual brilliance. Warton was fascinated by the man, and lay watching and listening throughout the morning.

In the afternoon, Savage and Ryeward arrived, their pockets bulging with cigarettes and books. Warton inquired eagerly as to what had happened on the morning patrol, and was relieved to hear that he had not missed much seeing that no Huns had been encountered. Shortly after, the major walked in and sat down at the foot of Warton's bed.

'Well, you are an old lead-swinger!' he began jovially. 'I've just been talking to the M.O. fellow, and he says that a week or two at Wimereux ought to give that scratch time to heal and buck you up again. So I'm going to send you both down there, probably in a few days' time, when you're fit to be moved.'

The days passed quickly enough, reading, talking, and going for occasional short walks round the camp, but the nights were interminable from lack of sleep. Warton made good progress, save that he became restless, and his speech developed a hesitation almost amounting to a stammer.

On the fifth day after they had been hit, he and Lastor were wrapped up in flying coats and put into the major's car that was waiting outside the camp. They both felt sorry to say good-bye to the sister, and they promised to visit her when they returned to the squadron. When they entered the squadron mess, every man came forward and drank to their speedy recovery. Warton was surprised to realise how little he knew about these men. In the past he had been so content with his own particular friends, that they had hardly entered into his life at all. He and Lastor gathered together some clothes and books from their hut, and continued their journey to Boulogne. Two hours later they had passed through the town and were climbing the long cliff road that leads to Wimereux. The hospital had once been a hotel, and, with its terrace, its long corridors, and, above all, its bathrooms, afforded pleasant contrast to the cramped space and makeshift arrangements of a Nissen hut. Lastor's foot had soon healed sufficiently to enable him to limp about with the assistance of a stick. The wound in Warton's shoulders also was closing well, and so, after the morning's examination by the M.O., they were free to wander round the neighbourhood or to take the tram into Boulogne until dinner time. The weather was perfect, day after day exhibiting cloudless skies and the faint horizon mist that promised more heat. During his stay in hospital, Warton got to know Lastor better than he could possibly have done in the squadron, and the better he knew him, the more he admired the serenity of outlook and defiance of circumstance that were his chief characteristics. On two occasions Savage and Ryeward came down to Boulogne in a tender to give them news and lunch with them. On other days they explored the shops, laying in a store of silk socks against the time when they should return to England, or else lay on the cliffs, watching the leave boats go out, and building plans for the future. It was arranged that they would shoot down a few more Huns, then return to England and get to the same training squadron, where Warton was to teach Lastor to fly. At the end of a fortnight, they persuaded the doctors that nothing could do them more good than a little flying, and so obtained permission to wire to the squadron for a tender. Instead of a tender, the C.O.'s car arrived with Savage and Ryeward full of enthusiasm and pleasure at the prospect of taking them home. 'Cheero, boys!' Savage greeted them. 'So you've got tired of leading an idle life, and are going to return to your languishing comrades. As on a previous occasion, I have taken the liberty of engaging a table at Mony's. We will proceed thither forthwith.'

Over the soup, Warton noticed three stars, carefully tarnished to make them look old, that ornamented each shoulder of Savage's tunic. 'Well, I'm darned!' he exclaimed. 'Why do you always wait to display your new and shining honours until we're having dinner at this place? First your ribbon, then this! Please explain.'

'The explanation is simple enough,' answered Savage, trying to speak carelessly, but only partially succeeding. 'Fories went home two days ago, and they've given me his flight. By the way, he was sorry he couldn't look you up, but he was too busy.'

'So this silly ass is now our flight commander!' interposed Ryeward, opening his lips for the first time.

The remainder of the dinner was spent discussing the new development, and the possibilities of the flight. 'What I first want to do,' said Savage, counting the items on his fingers, 'is to teach the beggars to fly; none of them know anything about it at present. Then to fly in formation; then to learn the country; then to recognise a Hun when they see one; and, finally, to shoot him down when they do recognise him. All that will take time, and meanwhile, I suggest, Warts, that you and I, with the co-operation of our skilful observers, do voluntary two-machine shows for the express purpose of confounding all Huns of every size, shape, manner, and description, that defile the heavens by their presence. No; I'm speaking seriously now. Is it a bargain?'

'It is,' replied Warton fervently. Then the four leant across the table and put their heads together to discuss ways and means of attack, until the lights went out as a hint that it was time for them to leave the restaurant.

CHAPTER X

Catastrophe

On their arrival at the camp, which was greeted by much yelling and cheering, a number of excited individuals seized Warton and carried him into the mess, where he was forced to sit in a very dazed condition upon the table. An air-raid was in progress at the time, so the electric light from the workshop lorry had been cut off, and the room was only illuminated by a candle mounted in the neck of an empty bottle. The flame, set flickering by a draught, threw long, dancing shadows and revealed strange expressions on the men's faces. Puzzled to find a meaning in all this uproar, Warton stared smiling at the major, who was advancing towards him with a great display of solemnity. Still at a loss for a clue, he sat perfectly still while the major pinned to the lapel of his tunic an enormous M.C. ribbon, consisting of a strip of blanket with a bar of violet ink running down the centre.

'Telegram from Brigade dated the fifth inst.,' intoned the major, 'announces the award of the Military Cross to Lieut. J. Warton for–' He was interrupted by Warton, who jumped from the table and bolted through the door, intending to barricade himself in his hut. But he was restrained by Savage and dragged back. It was late in the night by the time he went to bed. On the first occasion that he saw himself in a mirror, with the decoration sewn beneath his wings, he was obliged to suppress a smile of satisfaction; but after two days the ribbon appeared no stranger than the wings themselves.

Under the command of Savage, 'A' flight found itself compelled to live more energetically than had ever been necessary while Fories had led them. Being himself a most finished pilot, an excellent shot, and wise beyond his years in his recognition of the importance of work, Savage chased his men up into the sky when they had rather been playing ping-pong, or led practice formations when the weather was too bad for even a line patrol. At this, some grumbled openly until his sarcasm beat them into silence. But the value of his training was made manifest when, with a formation of six, as against the four that Fories had usually handled, he destroyed nine machines and a balloon on one patrol. The fact that not one man during that morning's fighting lost his position in formation, or placed himself in a dangerous situation, gave ample testimony to the discipline with which he controlled his flight. 'A' flight was proud of itself, for every pilot in the flight, after being led by Savage for a fortnight, had shot down at least three enemy machines, and, moreover, had an excellent chance of surviving his six months in France. From being dissatisfied with the incessant practice flying, they became enthusiastic, and at every minute of the day some machine of 'A' flight might be seen diving on the target, or having its guns tested on the range. The success of his methods was reflected by the mechanics, who took a greater pride than ever in the particular machine for which they were responsible and the number of Huns accounted for by its pilot. It was an almost unheard-of event for an engine in Savage's flight to fail in the execution of its duty.

Whenever he was not flying, Savage worked in the sheds, superintending the rigging of his machines, or making small improvements in the cockpits and gun-mountings. At the end of ten days he knew the family history of each man, and most of their personal ambitions.

Warton, during this period, had done no flying over the lines, as the major considered that he needed a rest. However, he assisted Savage with the ground work, and with the training of new pilots in the air.

When, eventually, he obtained permission to resume war flying, he fastened the single streamer of a deputy leader to the rudder of his machine, and followed Savage with the enthusiasm of one week's active service combined with the experience of six months.

After a few days' flying, he began to understand the secret of Savage's success, and to realise that it was not only knowledge of aerial tactics and the use of sun and clouds upon which he relied, but also upon knowledge of the German pilot. The Huns always seemed to do what Savage wanted them to, while of tricks and ruses he had no end. In the course of three weeks' flying, Savage never made one mistake in leadership, and his flight added another eighteen enemy casualties to its list. 'I haven't made a mistake yet, old son,' Savage remarked one day, pensively; 'but when I do, it'll be the finish of me.'

Instead of moving into the flight commander's hut with Dawson and Colley, who held 'B' and 'C' flights respectively, he insisted on remaining in his old hut with Warton and Lastor. This decision received particular approval from Ryeward, who was almost genial throughout an entire evening on account of it. As the days passed, Warton noticed that Savage very rarely got a good night's rest, and that in the morning his eyes were underlined by dark semicircles, while his manner was abrupt and irritable. On one occasion, his little terrier, Blackie, jumped upon his chest while he was asleep. Savage started like a scared rabbit, and hurled Blackie across the hut with an oath consigning him to the devil. The terrier yelped and stood regarding his master reproachfully. 'I'm sorry, Blackie,' said Savage, picking him up and pulling his ears, 'but you oughtn't to mind going to the devil, for the devil is the only immortal that has preserved his sense of humour. Recommend me to hell, Blackie, where a man may talk without fear of treading on his neighbour's religious corns. Furthermore, Blackie, remember that virtue may be tolerated for a lifetime–I repeat *may*–but not for eternity.'

Warton, who had been listening to this soliloquy from his bed, judged it time to interrupt.

'Why all this philosophy so early in the morning?' he inquired.

'I wasn't talking philosophy,' Savage replied. 'Philosophy consists of denying the existence of all that is most obvious, including the devil.'

'That, no doubt, is meant to be an epigram!' said Warton sarcastically.

'Certainly. Couch a confused thought in obscure language, and the result is an epigram.'

'And the answer's a lemon!' Warton interposed, laughing and stretching until a sharp pang reminded him of the newly-healed scar in his shoulder. 'Hell!' he ejaculated, whereupon Savage started to hum 'Home, sweet home.'

Savage got out of bed, rested his head on his hands, and stared morosely at Warton. 'A still, small voice whispers in mine ear that to-day is going to be a disastrous day,–a veritable *Dies Iræ*,' he announced; 'I am probably "building up for a dose of Spanish flu." "What is life without love?" inquireth the poet. "Very desirable," I reply, "but not so desirable as life without influenza." If it isn't flu, it's a presentiment. That probably means that young Gibson is going to get himself shot down in flames. I hate these ardent inflammatory spirits, including mess whisky, which, by the way, is getting worse every day.'

However, the day, in spite of his forebodings, passed off successfully enough, for he and Warton, in the course of their habitual two-machine patrols, each destroyed a Fokker triplane. This was the tenth machine that Warton had shot down, and Savage's fifteenth. On account of his excellent work, Savage was recommended for a bar to his M.C. A few days later, the bar was awarded to the Wing Equipment Officer, who had the same name, and who had won the Military Cross with the infantry. Savage affected to be much amused by the error, but his speech became even more bitter and sarcastic from that day. 'Decorations, my son,' he remarked grandly to Lastor, 'form an economical way of paying a man through his pride instead of his pocket. It is more politic to give a widow the cross her husband has won, than the amount of money he could have earned as a beggar in the streets.'

He formed a habit of starting nervously at every sound, and the major approached him on the subject of returning to England. 'Not at all necessary, sir,' answered Savage. 'I am merely practising so that when I go home I may win sympathy from the sentimental by playing the part of nerve-racked airman.' The major laughed, and decided to allow him another week before sending in his papers for Home Establishment.

Warton was getting very worried over Savage's condition, and taxed him with overwork. 'You know you can't keep it up, old man,' he said seriously. 'You're averaging about eight hours flying a day with all these practice formations and stuff, and you're making an absolute wreck of yourself. Look here, why not cut out these extra shows you do with me? You'll be going home soon, and neither of us really wants any more Huns. The flight's as good as any in France, so—'

Savage interrupted him by putting an arm round his shoulders. 'Say you're afraid I'll make some silly ass mistake and get us both done in, and be done with it!' he remarked.

'Don't be a fool!' Warton replied angrily. 'You know I think nothing of the sort.'

'Then don't worry about me. I'm going to fly until the hour before

I leave France, if I have to sweat blood from fear to do it. And remember, that if ever I do get you into a mess, I'll see that you get out of it all right.'

Warton grumbled further, but abandoned the argument.

For six days the routine of squadron life ran on as usual. Then one evening Savage got drunk. Warton was used to seeing men in various stages of intoxication, but Savage was by nature so abstemious that his condition appeared positively horrible. With Lastor's assistance, Warton undressed him and put him to bed, but, instead of falling into a stupor, as they hoped, Savage lay awake for many hours singing, and shouting, 'To-morrow I shall di-eee! To-morrow I shall di-eee!'

The following morning he apologised for the exhibition, saying: 'Sorry to have kept you chaps awake all night. Hope I didn't shock your susceptibilities by references to my horrible past. By way of reparation, Warts, I will follow your advice and take a day's rest. What is more, I'll take you with me. Gibson ought to be able to lead the flight for to-day, and it will be experience for him. Look here, I had a letter from a cousin of mine who's a V.A.D. or something at some place on the coast. Let's all go down to the sea and bathe, and try to get some of the girls for dinner. I'll borrow the major's car.'

It was with boisterous good spirits and the sense of having earned a holiday that the quartet set off on their journey. July touched woods and fields with hazy light, and the poplar trees that lined the road shimmered as the wind passed among their leaves.

Savage was in a better humour than he had been for many weeks. He took off his cap and leant back luxuriously in his seat. 'There is no doubt that motoring is the pleasantest form of travelling,' he said. 'Flying may be all very well for angels, and, I believe, it is also a popular pastime among the followers of Beelzebub; but for man, who is neither one nor the other, it is unsuitable—not to mention dangerous.'

'If that's your opinion, why don't you look after yourself better?' Lastor remarked.

'Nobody can look after himself,' replied Savage, 'any more than a sardine can choose the walking coffin which is to eat him.'

'Rot! Absolute rot!' Lastor exclaimed impatiently. 'Every one is as much master of his fate as he chooses to be.' Savage laughed.

'A rabbit squeaking in a trap is an exponent of freewill. A bullet directed by natural laws into the rabbit's brain is its answer. You can arrange nothing for yourself but the inevitable. Man is an excellent machine; let him be content with that.'

'Hic, haec; tekel upharsim!' replied Lastor rudely. 'If a free thinker were to preach a sermon he'd spout the same sort of bilge as you do, Savage.'

The argument was interrupted by Ryeward, who took little or no interest in such questions. 'Where are we going to get grub?' he asked. 'It's twelve o'clock and there isn't a pub for miles round.'

'Any old place'll do,' said Warton, 'so long as we can get an omelette and some wine.'

'Who are these girls we're going to see?' inquired Lastor. 'One of 'em's a cousin of yours, isn't she?'

'Wait and see, young Lochinvar,' answered Savage with a smile. 'The lady in question is hardly a cousin of mine, but I am engaged to her—or, anyway, shall be some day.'

'Shurr-up!' said Ryeward. 'Where do I come in?'

'Shall I propose to her for you?' Lastor suggested anxiously. 'Or shall we get Warton to sing outside her window? She'd elope with any one after hearing one verse!'

Savage did not trouble to reply, but busied himself with a pipe and an automatic lighter.

They arrived at Rue-sur-Plage by one o'clock, having refused to listen to Ryeward's vociferous demands that they should stop at an *estaminet* for lunch. Rue-sur-Plage was a small and not very pictur-esque watering-place that had been popular in days of peace for its bathing. It consisted of a nucleus of small shops and narrow streets, surrounded by a sprawling assembly of pretentious villas with stucco façades. At low tide the harbour was particularly smelly, for the water shrank into a narrow channel, leaving a green expanse of mud over which the seagulls screamed and wheeled. The streets were crowded with civilians and an enormous number of children who carried buckets and spades, and the usual seaside paraphernalia. But for the French soldiers sitting outside the cafes, and the deserted appearance of the casino, the town gave no testimony to the existence of war. A low-powered, antiquated aeroplane circled over the harbour, the observer standing perilously up on his seat, waving to the crowds below. Savage left his three companions in a darksome hotel where they proposed to lunch, while he went up to the hospital to find his 'cousin,' and make arrangements for the evening. A group of English girls on war service sat in a corner of the dining-room. They were remarkable for nothing save their short hair and a habit of addressing each other by their surnames, but Ryeward, after eyeing them speculatively for some time, had to be forcefully restrained from introducing himself. Savage was absent for a considerable time, and was greeted on his return by cries of 'Where have you been?' 'What have you been up to?'

Savage laughed shortly by way of reply. 'Had to spend some time congratulating my cousin on her recent engagement to one of the patients,' he said. 'Charming fellow. A.S.C. man with neurasthenia. None of the girls can come out to dinner, as they're giving some sort of entertainment at the Y.M.C.A., so I'm afraid the evening's a wash-out. Personally, I think a return to the aerodrome is indicated.'

Ryeward protested loudly against this proposal, but he was overridden by the others, and it was decided that they should return as soon as Savage had had something to eat. Noticing the hearty meal consumed by his pilot, Ryeward tactlessly remarked that his discovery had not apparently 'put him off his feed'. 'Why should it?' replied Savage. 'Eschew all emotion, my young friend, and you will eat with as hearty appetite as I. Pain consists of a morbid condition of the body; emotion, of a morbid condition of the mind. Behold me perfectly sound in mind and body. Furthermore, a good appetite is the outward sign of sound morals, for moral economy consists in the cutting down of emotional expenses.'

'The wise man speaks. Let us hearken unto his words!' said Lastor, folding his hands, and gazing into Savage's face with an air of rapt attention.

'Savage is a lump of conceited damn foolery!' Ryeward declared emphatically. 'He just opens a hole in his face and lets the hot air come out.'

When they were leaving Rue-sur-Plage, a small yellow mongrel ran across the wheels of the car. Its piteous yelps were mixed with the screech of the brakes, as the driver pulled up the motor almost in its own length. The four men got out and walked back to where a very old woman was bending over the twitching body on the road, and sobbing as though her heart were broken. Without clearly understanding a word she uttered, Warton got the impression that the dog had been the stay of her family, the comfort of her old age, and the object upon which she had lavished her entire affection.

Almost before they reached it, the mongrel was dead. All four stood round the woman, wondering what they should do, for, in the face of such grief, an offer of money seemed too sordid. Savage, however, pulled out his pocket-case and tentatively offered her a ten-franc note. As by a miracle, the old woman's tears were dried and her face exhibited a thousand new wrinkles as she smiled. Picking up the dog's body by its tail, she slung it into the ditch, then tottered back to her cottage, crackling the note between her fingers with every appearance of satisfaction. 'Cunning old crone!' remarked Savage, as they settled themselves in the car again. 'She knew well enough some fool would pay for her sobs. Philosophical, too! She takes life as it comes, yet doesn't scorn to make profit from it as it goes.'

After this incident they travelled in silence until they topped the rise whence the distant aerodrome could be seen as a cluster of huts and hangars on the summit of a hill. From out of the cloudless sky, a machine was spiralling down, the sun flashing on its wings at every turn. 'I'm going to fly this evening,' said Savage, suddenly breaking the silence.

> 'Wilt fly with me, oh valiant Warts,
> And strive to shoot a Hun down?
> For, methinks, we really oughts
> Kill somebody 'ere sun down!'

'Pretty good, that, for an improvisation.'

'Don't be a silly ass! Hanged if I let you fly to-day! Hallo! There's the major doing semaphore from the office. We'd better stop and see what's wrong.'

The major strolled across the road and leant against the door of his car.

'I didn't expect to see you people back so soon,' he observed. 'However, now you are here, you'll be able to carry out an idea of mine. Savage, your H.E. papers are through, and you'll be going home to-morrow, or at any rate the next day. I propose, therefore, to have a good dinner and binge to-night, to give you a send-off, and to inaugurate the reign of our new flight commander–Captain Warton. World without end. Amen!'

With a nod and a smile, the major left them in order to explore the cookhouse, and to threaten the cook with field punishment for all eternity if he allowed any caterpillars to be served with the vegetables that night.

Warton defended himself from the physical congratulations that were showered upon him by saying, 'Well, that settles your little scheme of going over the lines this evening, Savage.'

'It does!' replied Savage promptly. 'I shall leave the ground in quarter of an hour's time. Are you coming with me, Captain Warton?'

'Don't be a blasted idiot, Savage!' Warton retorted. 'You're going home to-morrow.'

'Besides,' added Lastor, 'it's beastly unlucky to fly the day before going on H.E.'

'Aha! My young apostle of freewill is converted to my theory of lucky impotence!' Savage shouted triumphantly. 'Good enough! Now I, for this evening, will adopt your philosophy and become master of my fate, and all the rest of it. Mark my words, whatever gods there be! To-night a Hun goes down, if I have to pull the beggar down with my own hands.'

All further arguments he turned aside with jokes and laughter, while he sent an orderly to his flight sergeant with instructions that the usual two machines should have their engines started. Very sulkily Warton changed his field boots for a pair of big fleece-lined thigh boots, and wound a long woollen scarf round his neck while Savage maintained an incessant flow of conversation.

'Cheer up, you two funeral mutes. Where the devil did I put my gloves? One more show, then Blighty and a month's leave! Dinners at the Savoy, Blackie, where you and I will feast like kings on a couple of meat coupons. Theatres, and perhaps a dance or two. Great Cæsar's ghost, why does that fool of a batman always throw my goggles under the bed! Meanwhile, Blackie, we go up for our last show! Buck up, all of you; I'm going over to get the engines run up.'

He departed, slamming the door and whistling villainously out of tune.

Once he was in the air, Warton's spirits rose, and he comforted himself with the thought that Savage was not likely to cross the lines, or that if he did, there was no reason to suppose that he would run into danger. It was part of Warton's flying creed that his leader never made a mistake. He flew very close to Savage, and almost abreast with him, while Lastor and Ryeward signalled to each other with their arms. Along the line there were no signs of activity save for an occasional shell burst. The air was dead calm and the horizon was encircled by a ring of vivid blue mist. They climbed steadily for an hour, much to Warton's annoyance, for he knew that Savage would never have troubled to climb 15,000 feet if it had not been his intention to cross the lines.

At seven o'clock they were well over the lines, dodging Archie bursts, and working their way gradually south. Evening mists rising from the ground, shrouded the west with layer after layer of golden gauze, through which canals gleamed or the forests showed sombrely. Windows from the towns in the east glittered like fireflies. On their own level, and flying into the west, Warton saw eight Huns, like white grains of wheat against the horizon. Long shadows thrown by the sinking sun darkened the earth, and he shivered. High above them in the north, hung a formation of many machines. One glance told Warton that they also were hostile, and he concluded that Savage under such circumstances, would never dare to attack the approaching eight. It was clear that they must get away north-west at once, if they wished to avoid an almost suicidal fight. But Savage turned east and flew to meet the enemy. Warton, realising that he could not have seen the formation in the north, dived, firing a red light so as to attract his attention. There was no answer from Savage's machine, for both he and Ryeward were concentrated on the approaching combat. Warton was desperate with anxiety, and cold with fear. Every second drew them closer into a situation from which there seemed no hope of escape. He knew that Savage was making a fatal mistake, but possessed no means of warning him. Again he pushed the throttle forward, but this time he did not overtake Savage, for the latter had already started his attack, and was diving into the formation below him. Warton looked once at the Fokker triplanes, where they hung overhead, circling and waiting, then he turned his back on them and followed Savage. Something fluttered brokenly downwards as Savage rose after his first dive, and wheeled to attack again. Warton was trembling violently, and missed his man. The Fokkers came down boldly enough, for the odds were all in their favour, and the two British machines were soon surrounded by streaks of blue smoke tracer that leapt at them from every angle. Warton settled down to fight and shoot, and his mind became a blank screen upon which alone was registered an impression of flashing wings and machines that climbed, attacked, and fell away. But always he kept close to the tail of his leader's machine, leaving his own to be guarded by Lastor. From time to time a Hun dropped flaming, or plunged devilishly into space below. The sky darkened, and he heard his ragged planes groan as they were racked by the strain of fighting. Lastor had long since expended all his ammunition, and hurled everything movable at his opponents. He now sat with his arms folded, watching Savage's machine, whence also there came no signs of gunfire. The two machines danced round each other, up and down in spirals and circles, dodging one German scout only to fly into the sights of another. Bullets did not come so thickly, for some of the Huns had fired every round they had, others were trying to remedy gun stoppages, while the rest were reserving their fire, waiting for a chance to kill. Yet it was only a question of time, as Warton knew, for the fight held them like a spell from which it was impossible to break away. The movements of flying, the combination of eye and muscle, had become so automatic that Warton had little consciousness of the events that were taking place around him. He was only tired, hopeless, and faintly anxious for the whole affair to be over and done with. Then he saw a triplane a few yards in front and above, that was dipping its nose until he could see along the engine-cowling into the muzzles of its guns. The thought flashed through his mind: 'He's got me!'

Across from the flank, down on top of the triplane, there rushed another machine. Warton had just realised from the streamers on its tail and a figure that stood up frantically waving in the back seat, that it was Savage, when, with a crash, the sight of which hurt him through every nerve in his body, the two machines met. Triplane and its attacker, mixed to form one indistinguishable mass of wreckage that fell, burning furiously. Heedless of every danger, Warton circled round and round the scene of the collision, watching the spark of fire grow fainter in the mists below until it was finally extinguished. When he looked up again, he was alone in the sky.

Beyond the western horizon the sun was disappearing behind a bank of scarlet-edged clouds; and as he flew towards it, Warton's lips were repeating over and over again one phrase: 'You silly ass! You did it on purpose!'

The Last Show

For a month after this incident, Warton led his flight on the usual patrols and escorts without sustaining any casualty, but also without any brilliant success. Savage had trained his men so well in formation flying and the elements of aerial fighting that Warton could find very little to teach them. He knew that under all ordinary circumstances they could be relied upon to look after themselves, and he carefully avoided any conflict which might put too great a strain upon their abilities.

Mechanical as his flying had become, he still took a pleasure in it. The fulfilment of his ground duties was irksome in the extreme, yet he attended to them conscientiously, though with a certain lassitude that was at once remarked by the major. 'That affair with Savage has knocked all the stuffing out of him,' he observed to the Recording Officer; 'I'll have to send him home in a week or two, or else he'll crock up completely.' Warton's pilots trusted him and admired his leadership. 'Old Warts is as safe as houses,' they said. 'Can't imagine him doing anything rash.'

With Lastor, he discussed Savage's death many times and at length, wondering whether the disappointment that Savage had met with at Rue-sur-Plage was in any way concerned with it. 'I don't think so for a moment,' Lastor maintained. 'Old Savage may have been a bit bored and so on, but he would never have run extra risk on that account, particularly as it involved Ryeward and us as well. No. I put the whole thing down to impulsiveness and obstinacy. You remember that it was just as we came in sight of the aerodrome that Savage said he was going up? That was just a passing impulse; but, when he heard that his H.E. papers were through, he persisted out of sheer obstinacy. As to the fight itself–well, all we can say is that Savage, for the first time in his life, made a bad mistake. He didn't see those Huns above us. When he found out what an awful mess he'd led us into, he fought until all his ammunition was gone; realised that it was simply a question of time before both of us got shot down; and then smashed into that Hun to give us a chance of clearing off. He knew that the sight would upset the Huns just as much as it did us, and he calculated on our getting away in consequence. Of course it meant killing Ryeward as well as himself, but then Ryeward would have been killed in any case, for the Huns would certainly have shot us both down. I'm absolutely certain that Savage thought the whole thing out, and used his brain up to the last second.'

'Jove! But he was a man!' exclaimed Warton softly.

Flying in England afforded Warton little prospect of success, for his manner was not ingratiating, nor yet overbearing. He was accustomed to active service conditions, where less comment was excited by the destruction of an enemy formation than there was at home over a broken tail skid, or the loss of a cap to a petrol tin.

He lived for the day and its work, without thoughts of the future or the past.

After three weeks, Lastor was awarded the M.C., while Warton received a bar to his, whereat he was not a little surprised. He laughed as he pinned the little ornament to his tunic. 'Net gain from my visit to this country,' he said; 'a ribbon, a rosette, and a rotten bad temper!'

He thought considerably about his career in France, and decided that it had been a most unusual one. Every other man in the squadron was at any rate on friendly terms with his companions; he knew them all by name, but no more. He had never participated in the ragging and singing, the ping-pong and card playing, indulged in by the members of the squadron night after night. Savage had laughed at them all for a pack of cheery, well-meaning schoolboys, and unconsciously Warton had adopted the same attitude. A society in time of war, as in peace, readily splits itself up into numerous small cliques, each dominated by the strongest personality. Savage had held such a position with regard to Warton, and now, in his absence, Warton felt as much at a loss as a dog without its master.

He came to rely more and more on Lastor for companionship, conversation, and even for opinions. Lastor, like Savage, had as his chief characteristic self-confidence, but he derived it from a very different source. Savage was self-confident because in his blind fatalism he imagined that Fate would deal kindly by him; Lastor, because he denied the existence of Fate, and put unlimited trust in his own powers. Warton, who had been forced from boyhood into manhood by the experiences and responsibilities of a few weeks, was as yet too uncertain in his ideas to be able to construct a philosophy for himself. In one respect only did he maintain a conscious superiority to Lastor, and that was in his skill as a pilot; illogically, therefore, it became his chief ambition to teach Lastor to fly. The Quartet had been unsociable to the squadron in the past for individual reasons; Warton because he was shy; Savage, because he ridiculed all men; and Lastor, because he was entirely self-contained. Ryeward was by nature so taciturn that any form of intimacy with him had been impossible.

By degrees, under the influence of Lastor's imperturbable views on life, and carefully concealed energy, Warton came to take a new interest in his work. He reviewed his past achievements and his talents; the destruction of twenty-three German machines, and a happy knack of shooting straight. Anything he might acquire in the future must result from his knowledge of aerial fighting and careful use of a machine-gun. At first vague, but growing steadily in purpose and intensity, came the desire to gain further recognition and win another decoration. The chances seemed all in his favour, for he knew himself to be an expert in the handling of a fighting machine, and, with Lastor as observer, he felt that nothing short of overwhelming odds or inevitable bad luck could defeat him. If he could count upon staying overseas for an indefinite period, the decoration would come to him in the ordinary course of his work, for he rarely went into a fight without bringing one of his opponents down; but with the prospect of being laid on the shelf in England so close before him, he realised that some action of outstanding brilliance and merit would be required. Such an action involved unforeseen consequences, and for a long time he debated in his mind whether to take the risk; but the desire to see D.S.O. written after his name was so strong that the result of that debate was almost settled in his own mind before ever he had started it.

Thereafter he flew with a new enthusiasm, and faced the world with a curious air of suppressed triumph. The major quickly noticed his change in manner, and was puzzled by it. He discussed the matter, as was his custom, with Astley. 'I can't understand that fellow,' he said thoughtfully, watching Warton as he strode whistling past the squadron office. 'A few weeks ago he was going about looking like Hamlet in flying clothes. Now he's as pleased with life as a cherub possessed of the devil. He doesn't buck himself with drink, does he?' he added anxiously. Astley handed him a small slip of paper.

'No, sir,' he said. 'Look at his mess bill.'

The major frowned and tapped the paper with his fingers as though he were disappointed with it. 'Hm!' he said at length. 'He's a fair whale for lime juice, and that's about the worst one can say about him. Anyway, he seems to have got his nerve back.' The major turned to the consideration of a pile of papers that lay upon his desk, and left the problem of Warton's new behaviour unsolved.

For some time past there had been rumours of a move to another aerodrome on the same part of the front, but closer up to the lines. The major had maintained a discreet silence on this subject, but it was felt that his silence was ominous, and groups of men in the mess whispered darkly of an approaching offensive, of extra shows conducted from a base within shelling distance of the line, of an aerodrome pitted with bomb holes, where they would be required to sleep under canvas and land their machines cross wind. At length the name of their destination was divulged, and Warton flew over to inspect their new quarters. He discovered that to a certain extent the squadron's fears had been well grounded, for the aerodrome, although unmarked by pits, was small and unsuitable, while the prospective site of the officers' quarters consisted of a virgin cornfield swarming with insects. The hangars were new, but there was no transport accommodation, and the nearest water supply was in a village more than a mile distant. With the help of some engineers, the ground was cleared, tents erected, and a rough lorry park constructed. Then the squadron moved in, execrated the wilderness in appropriate terms, and proceeded to make itself as comfortable as possible. Floor boards for the tents were in great demand, and Warton, having secured a supply for himself and Lastor, marked them with chalk and gave strict injunctions to his batman that they were not to be touched. Five minutes later, he observed a rival batman, who had been patrolling the camp with a speculative eye, emerge from his tent, glance cautiously about him, and then sidle rapidly away with the floor boards, which he deposited in the tent next door. Later in the evening, Warton discovered his boards in the tent farthest removed from his own, and carried them back to their original resting place.

He was sharing a tent with Lastor. When their camp beds had been fixed up, and kit unpacked, they set to work digging a trench outside the canvas, and spraying the surrounding grass with Pyrene to kill the insects. But at night they discovered that the tent was still infested with insects, mostly earwigs, which crawled up the sloping walls into the apex, whence they fell in showers whenever the canvas was shaken. Large spiders also, with long delicate legs, inhabited the dark corners or installed themselves between the blankets. Lastor fed them on insecticide, which they seemed to consider both palatable and nutritious. At intervals throughout the night, Warton started up with a yell to brush an earwig from his face, or extract a reluctant spider from the jacket of his pyjamas. He had not slept soundly for several weeks, but on this occasion he lay awake till dawn, counting the things both real and imaginary that were creeping over his body. For a week the men laboured erecting wooden huts for the squadron office, the armourers' hut, and the headquarters' workshop. A keen system of honest thieving was instituted, whereby the material for each hut was used for the construction of its neighbour. On the day that the armourers' hut was completed, it was irreparably wrecked by a machine which landed on its roof. The pilot was unhurt, but that fact did not serve to abate the Armament Officer's fury.

Owing to the insects and the heat, Warton never obtained more than three hours' sleep a night, and frequently none at all, for, in the early morning, when he usually fell asleep from sheer exhaustion, a party of Chinese labourers, employed on the Nissen huts for the mess, started work to the accompaniment of hammers rattling on iron, and a peculiar cheerful howling.

Every day when he was over the lines, Warton searched the sky and the earth for an opportunity to distinguish himself, but he was determined that his flight should not participate in the danger. The routine and humorous incidents of life on the ground amused him, yet, at the back of his mind there remained, strong and persistent, the desire for another decoration.

Instead of the offensive patrols which had formerly been allotted to 'Vic' squadron, they were now required to escort bombing raids, carried out by a large number of machines from a low altitude. The usual objective of these raids was a German aerodrome. Operating in conjunction with the bombers and escort, there was always a large number of single-seaters, who descended to within a few hundred feet of the ground, and used their machine-guns to supplement the effect of the bombs. Warton enjoyed these raids, for the Germans always attacked in large formations, and afforded the escort unusual chances for aerial manoeuvres. The conclusion of each raid presented the same aspect, a conflicting mass of British and German machines that fought round each other like gnats in a sunbeam, from 14,000 feet down to the ground. Warton, with his formation of five machines close behind him, was master in a mixed fight of this description, able to go where he pleased, and do what he pleased, for the Germans, while flying together in swarms, always fought as individuals.

It was in the course of a raid on Soulée aerodrome, where the Germans kept their big night-fliers, that Warton's opportunity came to him. Dusk was closing in, and the machines were gathering together in their formations for the journey home. In the east, a few persistent Huns were making half-hearted attacks on stragglers, but the majority had already dived away and disappeared. Warton's attention was caught by a white light fired from a small single-seater flying just in front and below him. From the signal of distress, he judged that the scout pilot was having trouble with his engine, and was asking for an escort to protect him from marauders. He gathered his formation about him and crept up to within a few yards of the scout, whose pilot waved a hand at him to signify that it was impossible for him to glide back over the lines. Then Warton realised that they were twenty-five miles into enemy territory, and that with only five thousand feet of height there was no alternative for the scout pilot but to land and give himself up as a prisoner of war. Warton looked at the slowly-revolving propeller of the distressed machine, at the western horizon, and then at the ground below him. It was good, open country, and apparently suitable for landing. Impulsively he throttled the engine back, and turned to shout at Lastor: 'I say! Shall we go down and give this fellow a lift home?'

'Right–e–oh!' returned Lastor, without a trace of excitement.

'Fire a green light, then,' Warton continued. 'Gibson can take the rest home.'

When the report of the pistol rang out, and the green light curved hissing up into the air, Warton knew himself to be committed to the adventure. Unwinkingly he watched the light, as it fell star-like towards the earth; then suddenly pulled himself together, realising that he was wasting valuable time. He shut off his engine, and glided down, keeping close to the scout. His five companions flew round in circles over his head, watching. With a new concentration, Warton stared at the ground, studying its every feature, rejecting one landing-place on account of its approach, another on account of its surface, a third because of its proximity to a main road. There were many qualifications to be possessed by the site he chose for his landing if he were to be successful. It was to be removed from any cottages, or camp, or thoroughfare, to give him time to pick up the scout pilot and leave the ground again before any Germans could come upon him. It must be a natural aerodrome on the level, possessing a low boundary and hard surface, for a bad landing, involving a strained undercarriage, would mean a prison camp for him as well.

Warton leant far out over the side of his machine, turning these different points over in his mind, until he had selected a suitable field, registered the direction of the wind, and mentally prepared every turn of his approach. He tested his engine in order to keep it warm, and dived below the scout so as to gain the lead. In the back seat, Lastor, humming softly to himself, selected a double drum of ammunition for his gun, and swung the mounting, before he settled down to watch Warton negotiate his landing. Not a sign of life could be seen on the earth. Mists rising from the lowlands faintly blurred their edges, making them look as though they had been rubbed with sandpaper. Warton had chosen a big square of yellow stubble where the corn had been cut. It was easy to judge for landing, because the nearest trees lay along a road over a mile to one side, but he considered it would be almost inaccessible from the ground, as it was enclosed on three sides by standing corn, and on the third by a small stream. Running parallel to one side of the square, but some distance from it, there seemed to be a track where the corn had been beaten down. Using his engine to bring him in low down over the stream, Warton flew towards the stubble. He throttled back and played gently with the joy-stick as the ground streamed past close underneath his wings. The shock-absorber on his wheels grunted once; then the machine rolled itself to a standstill. Warton, who had been holding his breath for thirty seconds past, gave vent to a long sigh of relief. He had landed safely in Hun-land, and thus accomplished the first part of his adventure.

All that now remained was for the scout to land, its pilot to jump into his machine, and then for all three of them to fly away together. He had taken three up before and had no fear that his engine would fail him. Immediately after landing, he had taxied his machine into a corner of the square and swung it into the wind, ready to take off immediately. Less than a thousand feet up now, the scout was side-slipping away his height and measuring his distance to the open patch. Warton fingered the chin-strap of his helmet, and glanced at the watch–six-thirty. It was barely four minutes ago that he had seen the white signal light, yet he could have sworn it was half an hour. He turned round to mention this fact to Lastor, but discovered him with one hand on the gun staring fixedly at a number of minute figures that were running towards them along the track through the corn. 'Huns!' said Lastor simply, and gave the magazine on his Lewis gun a pat. Warton said nothing, but opened the throttle of his engine a trifle, and anxiously watched the little scout, now only a few feet from the ground, and floating along the stubble towards the corn.

'He's going to overshoot!' shrieked Warton, suddenly jumping up in his seat. 'Oh! The fool! The fool! There he goes! Bang into the corn!'

As he spoke, the scout, which had allowed rather too much height for the approach, was caught by the tough stems which wrapped themselves round its wings and undercarriage. The machine stood up on its nose, shattering the propeller, crashed over suddenly on to its back, and burst into flames. At once Warton's anger was turned to solicitude. He jumped out and ran towards the blazing wreck, calling to Lastor the while; but the rattle of Lastor's machine-gun was the only answer he received. The scout pilot was pinned by both legs under the petrol tank. His clothes were burning on his body, and he lay beating the grass with his hands, screaming incoherently. Warton plunged into the mass of burning petrol and strained at the broken wood whose weight was holding the man down. Little tongues of flame caught at his face, peeling off the skin. Repeatedly he had to stagger back and beat his smouldering leather coat. Large beads of sweat stood out on his forehead, and he gasped for breath. An indescribable stench filled the air. Bit by bit, as the weight was raised, the man on the ground pulled himself free, until finally he rolled away and lay motionless and silent. Choked and half-blinded by the smoke, Warton groped his way to the shapeless bundle, one of whose charred flying-boots was still glowing by the wreckage. The heat of the body as he hoisted it on to his shoulder scorched him, and the indescribable smell followed him as he staggered back to his machine. Lastor's face was covered with blood, and one arm hung limp by his side. Several rents gaped in the fabric, and the cowling was bullet-splashed. With infinite relief, Warton noticed that the engine was still running. 'Here, Lasts!' he gasped. 'Haul this man up quick and let's get away! Oh, let's get away! For God's sake, let's get away!'

'All right, man! All right!' answered Lastor's calm voice. 'Don't get nervy. There; that's right now. I've got his shoulders. Push him up by his feet. Oh! Sorry, old man! I didn't notice. I've been having no end of a scrap with a bunch of Huns who are lying down over there in the corn. I couldn't come and help you, or they'd have nabbed the pair of us. As it is, they daren't poke their heads up. All right; I've got him in now. Nip up into your seat, and we'll show these devils a—Oh!—Warts!'

The last words accompanied the sound of a rifle shot fired from the neighbouring corn. Lastor, who had been kneeling on the fuselage helping to settle the injured man in his seat, lurched backwards, swaying; then, as another report rang out, crashed headlong from the machine on to the ground.

Unbelieving, Warton knelt down beside him. Both bullets had got home; the first through the body, the second in the head. Warton lifted the head between his hands and stared at it, with his lips open. He let it fall again, and rose to his feet with one exclamation: 'Explosive bullet!' Wearily he climbed up to his seat. Bullets flew whining past him, but he never heard them. For a few seconds he sat staring at Lastor's body. Then he pushed the throttle lever forward, and the machine skimmed roaring over the stubble into the air. Twice he circled the field on which lay the charred remains of an aeroplane and a small black speck. Then he flew into the darkening west, unheeding the passage of time until a rocket trembling and twinkling through the mist below drew him down on to his home aerodrome.

When they lifted the scout pilot from the back seat of his machine the body was already stiff and cold.

· · · · · ·

Six nights later, the major gave a dinner to celebrate the award of a second bar to Warton's M.C., and the occasion of his return to England on the following day. When the men had finished singing, 'For he's a jolly good fellow,' Warton was no longer in the mess. He crossed the road to the hangars, and crept into the one where his machine stood. The canvas flapped and the ropes creaked. Through an opening near the roof shone a clear, starlit sky, in whose light the propeller and wings of the aeroplane glowed faintly. For a long time Warton stood staring at the powerful, eager shape. When he was outside the hangar again, his eye was caught by the gun-flashes dancing along the east, as on the night when he had joined the squadron. Slowly he turned his back on them, and stumbled through the darkness to his tent.

Combats in the Air

While *Over and Above* is ostensibly a work of fiction, it is based on John Gurdon's experience with 22 Squadron in France over the spring and summer of 1918. The reader may therefore find an account of the squadron over that period a useful and interesting supplement to the text.

Once his training as a Bristol F.2b pilot was completed, John Gurdon was sent to France and to a pilot pool, to await a posting to an appropriate squadron. That meant waiting for the loss of a pilot in one of the few Bristol F.2b squadrons operating in France. These were 11, 20, 22, 48, and 88. The Bristol Fighter was a very popular machine to those who flew it in combat. It was fast, over 100 mph, with a surface ceiling of 20,000 feet and an endurance of three hours. The two men of its crew were situated close together in separate cockpits, which made communication between pilot and observer/gunner easy. The pilot had one fixed Vickers .303 machine gun firing through the propeller blades, while the observer had one, sometimes two, Lewis guns (depending on the man's physical strength) on a Scarff ring mounting. With that arrangement he could command a field of fire of

180 degrees to the rear, making sure he did not hit the aeroplane's tail fin in the process. Handled in an aggressive manner, an F.2b could take on any of the German air service's aeroplanes. A good rear-man would enable his pilot to concentrate on anything ahead of the aircraft, secure in the knowledge that an attack from the rear would be safeguarded by his crew member.

When the Bristol F.2a first appeared over France, with 48 Squadron in April 1917, its crew's first tactic was to form a tight group when threatened, trusting that any attackers would have to face the barrage of fire from numerous observers. This failed dismally, and it soon became apparent that the crews should engage in combat in the same manner as single-seater scouts, but with the added assistance of the man in the rear-facing cockpit.

A 22 Squadron crew was lost on 30 January 1918, shot down by Oberleutnant Harold Auffarth of Jasta 29, his eighth victory of an eventual twenty-nine. It seems likely that the loss of Bristol Fighter C4832 prompted the request for a replacement pilot from the pool, and John Gurdon was on his way.

The squadron was based at Treizennes, on the south-east outskirts of Aire and about five miles south-east of St Omer. The commanding officer, or CO, was Major L.W. Learmont DSO MC CdG, and he had been so since January 1917. Gurdon was posted to 'A' Flight, commanded by Captain F.G.C. Weare, a Sandhurst man, from Tunbridge Wells, Kent. For his first few days Gurdon merely stooged about, getting some more flying hours in his logbook, but he was eventually put on the flying schedule for operations.

Meanwhile, he began to become acquainted with his fellow pilots and observers. Among them was 2/Lt S.A. Oades MC, from south-east London. A former Royal Engineers sapper, he had been out with 22 Squadron since the autumn of 1917 and had already accounted for a number of enemy aircraft. On March 5th, Oades and his observer, 2/Lt S.W. Bunting, got into a scrap with enemy machines and although they claimed two, they had their propeller shot off. Both men were wounded but got down safely. Stan Bunting, from Ealing, had brought his score to seven, but it was the end of his flying career.

On the following day, 2/Lt G.W. Bulmer with 2/Lt S.J. Hunter shot down a Pfalz Scout 'out of control' (OOC). George Bulmer was born in Toronto, of American parents, and had settled in Canada. His claim was the first of nine he would score to win the Military Cross.

These OOC victories were in reality what were referred to as 'probables' in World War Two. As almost all air fights occurred over German-held territory, i.e. on the other side of the front-line trenches, British crews did not have the luxury of downing enemy aircraft west of the lines. Therefore, if a pilot or crewman felt certain he had hit a German aircraft, which then began to spin or dive down in a fashion that appeared it would crash – and provided it was similarly observed by either another pilot or a ground (army) observer – it was credited as an 'out of control' victory. It follows, of course, that most of these Germans merely spun or dived away from the action and went home, but it was the system in vogue when all things military in the air was still being learned. It follows, too, that a British airman who similarly spun or dived out of a sticky situation also pulled out lower down and went home. They must have known that a number of their OOC claims did not result in the destruction of an enemy. As German records do not appear to contain any list of German aircraft crashes in which the pilot survived, it is difficult for historians to tie events together. The only records that do survive are of airmen either killed or wounded. Nevertheless, an enemy aircraft forced down out of a battle was a form of moral victory.

On March 7th, Major Learmont was wounded. COs were not supposed to fly on operations at this stage of the war, their value being to command, but a number did. He engaged a German two-seater and was injured for his trouble, but he got back to the airfield safely. He was replaced by Major J.A. McKelvie.

Another pilot who became well known to Gurdon was W.F.J. Harvey, from Portslade, Sussex. (William Harvey, always known as Jim, later became Gurdon's brother-in-law.) Another former Royal Engineers man, he had arrived on 22 December 1917 and became a high-scoring pilot, although he did not make his first combat claim until 16 March 1918, a Pfalz that went OOC over Beaumont. His observer on this occasion was Sgt A. Burton, but Harvey's career was dotted with other observers during the summer.

Two days after Harvey's first claim, Weare and Lt G.S.L. Hayward crashed an Albatros DV Scout over Carvin. George Hayward also came from Tunbridge Wells, a former Royal West Kent officer. By the time he teamed up with Weare he had taken part in eleven successful combats, and with Weare would achieve a total of twenty-four, receiving the Military Cross. He later became a pilot, only to die in a crash in 1924.

On March 21st the Germans launched their spring offensive, Operation Michael, which managed to push a large area of the British lines back westwards, causing great upset. For some time the Royal Flying Corps (RFC) had been flying low-level bombing attacks on German troops and positions, and this now became more prevalent in an effort to stem the German incursion. The Bristol F.2b could carry up to twenty-four 20-lb Cooper bombs. 22 Squadron also took part in these operations, but the immediate reaction was for the squadron to move base, to Serny on the 21st and then to Vert-Galant two days later. Vert-Galant was much farther south, halfway between Doullens and Amiens.

On the 23rd, 22 Squadron lost two crews. On an offensive patrol (OP) to Cambrai, Capt P. Thompson and 2/Lt D.W. Kent-Jones were shot down. Thompson was killed and his observer was wounded and taken prisoner. On the same day 2/Lt H.L. Christie and Lt N.T. Berrington force-landed just inside British lines, where their machine, C4827, was destroyed by enemy shell fire. Vizefeldwebel Otto Könnecke of Jasta 5 was responsible for the second loss, while Jasta 69 may have downed Thompson.

Another airman Gurdon would have been well aware of was one of the few NCO pilots, Ernest John Elton. From Dorset, he had started his RFC career as an air mechanic with 6 Squadron. In fact he was a mechanic to one of the RFC's early heroes, Lanoe Hawker VC DSO. Elton eventually persuaded authority to allow him to train as a pilot and in early 1918 found himself with 22 Squadron. He and an observer claimed their first two victories on 26 February; by the end of March, their score had risen to sixteen – all in thirty-two days. Elton received the Distinguished Conduct Medal and Military Medal, while Italy conferred on him its Bronze Medal. George Hayward was his observer on six occasions, and finally, Lt R. Critchley.

Roland Critchley hailed from Lytham St Annes, Lancashire. He was credited with seven victories, all with Elton. As does Gurdon, Critchley appears in the famous photographic line-up of pilots and observers of 22 Squadron taken on April 1st, the day the RFC and Royal Naval Air Service merged into the Royal Air Force. On April 2nd, flying in A7286 with 2/Lt F. Williams, he met combat with Fokker Dr.I triplanes of Jasta 11 and was shot down and killed.

On the same day, Gurdon and 2/Lt A.J.H. Thornton claimed two Fokker triplanes shot down over Vauvillers, Gurdon's first victories. Anthony Thornton was six months younger than Gurdon and had joined the RFC in the autumn of 1917.

During April the squadron suffered a few casualties. Observer Lt B.C.M. Ward was wounded on the 6th, and 2/Lt H.F. Davison on the 13th. Hiram Frank Davison was a Canadian from Ontario who had transferred from the Canadian Horse Artillery to the RFC. During one of his first combats, on March 8th, he had seen the pilot of an Albatros Scout he was attacking fall from his cockpit. All his claims were in association with his observer, 2/Lt J.L. Morgan, from Caerphilly, Wales. The two flew many ground-attack sorties too, and both men received the Military Cross. They also appear in the April 1st photograph.

Two days after Davison was wounded another Canadian, 2/Lt G.N. Traunweiser, was killed along with Sgt S. Balding. Tragically it seems they were flying a low-level sortie and became the victim of British ground fire, in C4808. Traunweiser is also depicted in the celebrated photograph.

The next significant event for the squadron is shrouded in some mystery. In the early evening of May 7th, John Gurdon and Anthony Thornton, flying B1253 'E' in company with Lt A.C. Atkey MC and Lt G.C. Gass in B1164 'D', encountered seven enemy fighters and got into a scrap. The Germans were reinforced by around a dozen or so more, so the two British aircraft became mightily outnumbered. Their opponents were some of the new Fokker D.VII biplane scouts, the first anyone in 22 Squadron had seen in the air. Until now the German aeroplanes had all been Albatros or Pfalz scouts, or the nimble Fokker triplanes.

There is no doubt that the two British crews flew and fought desperately in the face of such odds, both by the front Vickers guns and the rear Lewis guns. The two Bristol Fighters eventually fought their way clear of what must have felt like certain death and returned to their airfield. When they reported what had occurred to the recording officer, it seemed that Atkey and Gass claimed two Fokkers destroyed, while Gurdon and Thornton claimed two more. When the dust settled, however, the score had risen to five to Atkey and three to Gurdon, making eight in all.

In the heat of battle, with everyone firing at each other as they twisted and turned, it is easy to overstate one's case. Nevertheless, the story held and naturally was picked up by Wing Headquarters and

An aerial oblique view of a corner of Vert-Galant aerodrome.

Lewis guns with Lewis and Vickers ammunition are issued to observers and pilots of 22 Squadron at the Vert-Galant aerodrome, 1 April 1918. Temporary 2/Lt Josiah Lewis Morgan talks to Armament Officer Lieutenant Shanks. To Morgan's right, 2/Lt Hiram Frank Davison looks on, shouldering a Lewis gun.

Air mechanics prepare a Bristol F.2b of 22 Squadron at Vert-Galant aerodrome, 1 April 1918. Part of the armament was a fixed Vickers gun inside the cowling, firing through the propeller. On the left is a group of pilots and observers in flying kit.

An observer in a Bristol Fighter of 22 Squadron with his dog at Vert-Galant aerodrome, 1 April 1918. Note the Scarff mounting, which was capable of carrying either a single or a twin Lewis gun.

An air mechanic hands a drum of ammunition for a Lewis gun to an observer in a Bristol F.2b of 22 Squadron, Vert-Galant aerodrome, 1 April 1918. The pilot is 2/Lt Davidson and the observer is 2/Lt Morgan.

A Bristol F.2b of 22 Squadron, Vert-Galant aerodrome, 1 April 1918.

A Bristol F.2b Fighter of 22 Squadron in flight over Vert-Galant aerodrome, 1 April 1918.

Men from 22 Squadron gathered at Vert-Galant after the squadron's historic first RAF flight on 1 April 1918. John Gurdon is on the wing, smoking a cigarette.

Pilots and observers of 22 Squadron hand over papers before going on patrol, Serny aerodrome, 17 June 1918. Emptying pockets was a precaution to prevent information reaching the enemy in the event of a forced landing. In the background are some Bristol Fighters of the squadron.

Bristol Fighters of 22 Squadron flying from Serny aerodrome in formation, 17 June 1918.

A Bristol F.2b of 22 Squadron in flight from Serny aerodrome, climbing to its position in the formation, 17 June 1918.

A four-gun Bristol F.2b of 22 Squadron, Agincourt. The squadron improvised the mounting for the top Lewis gun (one of three, with a Vickers as the fourth gun). The pilot is W.F.J. Harvey and the observer is D.E. Waight.

any journalistic people hanging about. The story was then expanded to become the renowned 'Two Against Twenty' air fight. That any German Jasta or Jagdgruppe would have lost eight of their fighters is hard to believe, and certainly nothing similar was ever reported. It must have been a case of the British quartet seeing several aircraft spin or stall away within the maelstrom, perhaps some exuding exhaust smoke from their straining engines, at which stage the heart saw what the eye didn't. This conclusion was solidified somewhat by war artist Joseph Simpson, who depicted the two Bristol Fighters surrounded by Albatros Scouts (not Fokkers), with the F.2bs' markings and serial numbers plainly in view. This drawing appeared in *The Sphere* magazine on June 29th, in a new feature by Boyd Cable, noted as 'Stories of the Air – No. 1'.

Following another successful day on May 9th, by which time Gurdon's score had reached nine or ten, his CO put forward a recommendation for an award. This resulted in the approval of a Distinguished Flying Cross, the new RAF decoration equivalent to the Military Cross. The citation was promulgated in *The London Gazette* dated 3 August 1918.

Oddly enough, Atkey did not receive any official recognition for his actions on May 7th, although he did later receive a bar to his Military Cross, although not gazetted until September. With the way of decorations, it may well be that because he had received the MC recently, another recommendation might not have been thought appropriate. Atkey and Gass claimed five more German aircraft shot down two days later, followed by a brace on the 15th, three on the 19th, and three more on the 20th. By June 2nd, Atkey's score was thirty-eight. As for Gass, he eventually received the MC in May but it was not gazetted until September. Thornton received nothing.

Arthur Clayburn Atkey came from Saskatchewan, Canada. Joining the RFC first as a bomber pilot, he flew DH4 bombers with 18 Squadron. Not content merely to bomb enemy targets, he and his observer were keen to engage hostile fighters, accounting for nine of them during the first few months of 1918. No doubt these aggressive tendencies led to his posting to the two-seat fighter outfit. He arrived on 22 Squadron in late April and teamed up with Charles George Gass, from Chelsea, London. Gass had been an NCO in France with 2/24th London Regiment. After Atkey returned to England in August, Gass flew with Gurdon.

It is also odd that John Gurdon did not include anything about this air fight in his book. Perhaps he realised that things had been blown out of proportion, more than likely by 'higher authority'.

On May 12th, 22 Squadron suffered another casualty, when 2/Lt C.E. Tyler and 2/Lt A.P. Bollins in B1162 were brought down by German anti-aircraft fire. Tyler got them down despite being wounded, but both were taken prisoner.

In June after some leave, Gurdon took on another observer, 2/Lt James John Scaramanga, who came from Redhill, Surrey. Scaramanga's first posting had been to 20 Squadron, where he was involved in two victories before being wounded on April 11th. He moved to 22 Squadron on June 6th.

In the meantime, Gurdon had been flying with Sgt Hall. On the morning of June 5th they ran into a two-seater observation machine, sending it down OOC. That evening they encountered fighters of Jasta 18. In this fight, north-east of La Bassée, Hall was wounded after Gurdon shot down a Pfalz D.III. It appears that Jasta 18 leader Leutnant Kurt Monnington brought down B1253, flown by Lt C.H. Dunster with Sgt L.A.F. Young. Young was killed and Dunster forced down wounded and taken prisoner. Leutnant Hebler claimed a second F.2b, but as it was not seen to go down on the German side he was only credited with a 'forced to land' inside British lines. This appears to have been Gurdon and Hall.

With Hall in hospital, Scaramanga took over in the rear cockpit for the rest of the month, although on June 23rd 2/Lt J. McDonald flew with Gurdon. James McDonald was a Scot from Renfrew, who had worked at a Post Office Savings Bank in London until he was old enough to join up. He was involved in eight successful combats – with Gurdon, George Bulmer, and Frank Gibbons – winning the DFC.

Elsewhere on the squadron, Jim Harvey and Lt A.P. Stoyle were shot up by Jasta 3 on June 18th. Harvey got them down on the right side of the lines, although C776 was wrecked. Oberleutnant Hermann Kohze, the Staffelfüher, was the attacker but his claim was not confirmed. Five days later Lt S.F.H. Thompson with Sgt R.M. Fletcher was shot up in a fight with Jasta 7. Samuel 'Siffy' Thompson, from Bow, London, was credited with thirty victories flying with 22 Squadron, flying with Ronald Fletcher for much of the time. Thompson received the MC and DFC, Fletcher the Distinguished Flying Medal for his involvement in twenty-six victory claims.

Then, on July 10th, Scaramanga was severely wounded. Flying in C1003 he and Gurdon took off at 0800 and fought several enemy aircraft, most of them Pfalz Scouts. Gurdon gives a good account of this action in *Over and Above*, detailing how the observer was hit and collapsed in his cockpit but struggled back to his gun in order to re-engage the enemy. Gurdon got them back to the aerodrome but Scaramanga died soon after. He was just short of his twentieth birthday.

The squadron was moved again on July 31st, this time to Maisoncelle, north-west of Hesdin. Gurdon was away from action until August, teaming up for his last few trips with Charles Gass. On August 8th, as the big Battle of Amiens began, Gurdon and Gass shot down an Albatros Scout in the morning, followed by another just afterwards, a victory shared with Jim Harvey and his observer, Capt D.E. Waight. Dennis Waight was another Londoner and a former fusilier officer, decorated with the MC. This combat was Waight's first but by the end of the war he had been involved in a dozen combat victories.

On August 27th, Lt F.M. Sellers and 2/Lt T B Collins, in E2514

'K' on a dawn patrol south-east of Arras, were shot down by Leutnant Hermann Frommherz of Jasta 27. It was the German's sixteenth victory of an eventual thirty-two, and a well-known photograph shows him in his room with the tail fin of the British plane nailed to the wall. Collins was killed and Sellers taken prisoner. Taking off a few hours earlier on the same day, Lt F.G. Gibbons and James McDonald had claimed a D.VII 'OOC'. Gibbons ended the war with fourteen victories, receiving the DFC. He was killed in a crash during an air race in 1932.

The last loss by 22 Squadron during Gurdon's time with it occurred on August 29th. During an OP along the Arras-to-Cambrai road, Lt J.J. Barrowman and 2/Lt J. Amos (E2453) were shot down. They had taken off at 0850 and were the victims of Vizefeldwebel Albert Lux of Jasta 27. This was Lux's fourth victory of an eventual eight.

August also closed out Gurdon's combat flying career. During a patrol, an anti-aircraft shell exploded close to his Bristol, causing him a concussion. This, together with an earlier injury that had been troubling him, persuaded the squadron doctor to recommend Gurdon's return to England as unfit for further operational flying. He arrived in September and relinquished his commission on 21 December 1918.

Norman Franks